Jury Pool

Sissy Marlyn

Copyediting by Robert Richie

BEARHEAD PUBLISHING

- BhP -

Louisville, Kentucky

EVIDENCE

Author *Sissy Marlyn*

Novel Number *One (in a trilogy of three)*

Date of Collection _____

Time of Collection _____

Collected By _____

Description of Evidence *A Fantastic Murder*

Mystery set in Louisville, KY

Location of Collection _____

_____

Type of Offense *Murder*

Victim(s) *Several!*

Suspect(s) *Uncovered by Reading Jury Pool!*

CHAIN OF CUSTODY

Received From_____

By _____

EVIDENCE

BEARHEAD PUBLISHING

- BhP -

Louisville, Kentucky
www.sissymarlyn.com

Jury Pool
by Sissy Marlyn
Copyediting by Robert Richie

Cover Design by Bearhead Publishing
First Printing - April 2006
ISBN: 0-9776260-2-4

Printed in the United States of America.

Acknowledgements

Thanks to the following individuals who kindly gave of their time and vast knowledge to make *Jury Pool* become a reality:

Robyne Ryan, Jury Manager – Jefferson County Courts

Pete Womack, MT (ASCP)

Ralph Miller, Police Chief, City of Shively

Sergeant Greg Brown, Criminal Investigation Section, Homicide Squad, Louisville Metro Police Department

Kirk and Leann – Petrus Restaurant and Nightclub

Other Novels Written by *Sissy Marlyn*:

Intimacies
Illusions
Indecisions

A trilogy of Women's Fiction Novels

For more information and synopsis of each novel, check
www.sissymarlyn.com

Prologue

A full moon and an array of brilliant, sparkling stars illuminated the night. A train thundered down the track, growing louder and louder, closer and closer. Renee Peterson stared into the blinding light on the front of the massive engine.

Vibrations from the track, and within her, jolted her body. Cold and clammy, sweat trickled down the back of her neck, pearled along the top of her chest and made her palms sticky. A piercing whistle pained her ears; a strong wind swept back her long hair. Her heart hammered, jarring her ribcage, pounding at her temples, and even reverberating in her dry, open mouth. Tears stung her eyes.

She heard the sickening screech of brakes, and she said one last prayer, "Lord, save me!" But knowing she would not live, her last thought was, *Lord, look after my husband and baby girl.*

She screamed at the top of her lungs as her body met with tons of steel. Her legs ripped from her body. Her torso rocketed off to the side and pounded into the side of a tree. A twisted, broken, gory mass – once her body – came to rest in a shallow ditch. Renee Peterson ceased to be.

Chapter 1

Suicide?

Monday morning – the first day of jury duty for a select group of men and women – over 200 people convened in the Jury Pool Assembly Hall, on the second floor of the Jefferson County Judicial Center, in downtown Louisville. In the front of the room, two, long, rectangular tables stood, with a few chairs behind each one, and a podium sandwiched in between.

A few men and women – busy executives from nearby companies – already resided at one of the tables. Hard at work, they clicked away on their laptops. Seated at the other table, a voluptuous redhead – Assistant Jury Manager, Jeanette O'Riley – checked off names of jurors as they entered the room. She also handed each person a badge with their assigned juror number on it. Each individual would be known by this number for the duration of their jury duty – two weeks.

Jeanette looked out over the room. Most of the potential jurors sat in padded, metal-framed chairs. Rows and rows of chairs spanned the large room. Ample florescent lights softly hummed overhead.

Out in the rows and columns of chairs, the familiar aroma of coffee permeated the air. Many quietly consumed this common morning brew, slowly waking up. Others hid their faces behind city and business newspapers and paperback novels. Still others chatted with strangers around them; some discussed what they did for a living; some complained about having to serve jury duty; some shared personal details about themselves. Many concurrent conversations of this type took place all around the room.

Jeanette scanned the room for the light purple, black and tan rectangular design of empty chairs. To those still standing around, she announced, "Ladies and gentlemen, there are still plenty of empty chairs. I'd like for you to have a seat, please. There's a work room in the very back. It contains another table and some chairs. To the left of this room is a coat room. There are even chairs located in this space. So there should be no need for anyone to stand."

Those standing quickly followed directions and sought out empty chairs. Carpeting on the floor kept the noise of shuffling feet to a minimum. A few moments later, at 9:15 a.m., a tall, skinny, dark-haired woman with glasses – Charly Donaldson – entered the room and stepped to the podium with a handheld microphone in her hand. In semi-casual dress, Charly and Jeanette, wore dress slacks and lightweight sweaters.

As those in the room noticed this other woman standing at the podium, they slowly quieted. "Good morning, everyone," the dark-haired woman's voice boomed through the microphone. "Welcome to the jury pool. We are glad to have you here, and we appreciate your willingness to perform your civic duty. Your time here makes possible the administration of justice. My name is Charly Donaldson. I am the Jury Manager. To my left is Assistant Jury Manager Jeanette O'Riley. Feel free to approach either of us with any questions you might have. Now, allow me to take a few moments to go over some important details about your time here. Fear not, if you do not take in all I say. That is why we have these informational pamphlets for each of you. Be sure and pick one up before you leave today."

Charly picked up a tri-fold brochure from the podium. She unfolded it and held it up over her head, displaying first one side and then the other. About to launch into her standard speech, she spied one of the deputy sheriffs entering the room. Two other gentlemen in suits, who Charly did not recognize, followed.

The deputies came and went often during the day, as they called potential jurors for different trials being formed that day. Still a bit early for this routine, the deputies did not usually have plain clothed men with them. *Something else must be up,* she assimilated.

"Charly, can Jeanette take over for you. These two gentlemen would like a word with you," Deputy Jordan told her.

Charly knew Deputy Jack Jordan well. A very nice older gentleman, he had a full head of wavy, carrot hair. His rounded stomach, which somewhat concealed the front of his belt, could be directly attributed to too many years of eating Dunkin' Donuts. Regardless of his extra weight, his holstered gun, handcuffs, and mace, as well as other various useful gadgets, showed around his sides and back.

"Of course, Jeanette can take over for me," Charly answered with an easy smile. "Jeanette, you know the drill," she said to her sidekick.

"Yes, I do," she agreed. She stood and stepped behind the podium, taking the microphone from Charly. She paused for only a second as she watched Charly leave the room with the deputy and the suits. Then she picked up right where Charly left off. "Let's begin with your term of duty…." she began.

As Jeanette rambled on with her speech, she glanced from time to time out the glass-paneled wall into the hallway.

Since the hallway side of the room was glass-paneled, the room resembled a fish bowl.

She saw a shocked expression appear on Charly's face as the men in suits told her something. Then Charly put her hands to her mouth as if she were stifling a scream. Anxious to complete her speech and go and find out what transpired with Charly, Jeanette rattled on, "Ladies, let me conclude by saying, if you feel you need an escort to your parking garage as you leave here each day, feel free to approach any of the deputies. An escort will be provided for you. Are there any questions?"

Jeanette paused and her eagle eyes scanned the room. No hands were raised. *Good!* She thought with relief. She wanted to be on her way. Curiosity about what Charly had learned was killing her.

"Alright, then," she said. "Call the number in your pamphlets before nine o'clock each morning to see if you are supposed to report and the exact time you are to be here. I'll see you again soon."

A few groans of dissention arose from the audience. Most everyone hated serving jury duty. Jeanette ignored the audience's grumbling. She turned and hurried from the room. Charly was still in the hallway, as were the deputy and the two suits. "What's up?" Jeanette wasted no time asking.

Charly held onto the wood railing at the top of a short, stucco wall that looked down on the first-floor lobby. She peered down from the second floor. As she released her hold and turned, Jeanette saw tears running down her face.

"Chars, what wrong?" Jeanette rushed to Charly's side and threw a strong arm around her shoulder, pulling her close.

"Jeannie, I...I don't know how to say this," Charly began in a shaky voice.

"Just say it," Jeanette prodded.

"It's Renee," she struggled to reveal. Without finishing, she began to sob.

Jeanette looked toward Deputy Jordan for some help, but he stared at his black polished shoes and shifted his weight from foot to foot. She focused her attention next on the men in suits. Her eyes caught sight of an older, stocky man with grey hair. His haphazard tie and his slightly wrinkled shirt and pants also held her attention for a second. Then she moved on to peruse the other gentleman – tall, slim and young with jet-black hair. His clothing impeccable – tie perfectly knotted, starched white shirt, unruffled black trousers – he almost appeared as if his mother dressed him. *A wet-behind-the-ears, twenty-something rookie*, Jeanette guessed.

"What's happened?" she questioned. Her demanding, sky-blue eyes darted from face to face, burning holes through the two strangers.

"Ma'am, I'm Detective Roger Matthews," the older gentlemen introduced, offering his hand. "And this is Detective Scott Arnold."

"And?" Jeanette inquired, impatient. Her fingers barely linked with the detective's. Not interested in pleasantries, Jeanette only wanted to know why these two gentlemen were there.

"We're...did you know Renee Peterson?"

Did I know...? A quiver ran up Jeanette's spine. She lowered her eyes from the detective's intense scrutiny. "Of course I know Renee. She's our office assistant. Why do you ask?"

Another moment of tense silence passed. Jeanette looked up into the detective's eyes once more. His eyes relayed sympathy. "Um...I'm sorry to tell you this, Miss, but we found Renee Peterson dead today."

"D...did you say...Renee's dead?!" Jeanette's eyes grew large and her lips parted. She placed her hand over her mouth. "Wha...what happened?"

"It appears she committed suicide," the detective relayed.

"What do you mean...it appears? What happened to her?" Jeanette continued, her questions becoming more pointed.

Charly pulled loose from her friend's grasp. She turned, clutched the railing again, and stared down at the tan, marble floor below. Her shoulders shook all the more. Her stomach churned. She could not bear to hear the detective relay the grisly details of Renee's death again. Having an awful time believing her assistant perished in such a horrible way, she tried her best to tune out the detective's next words.

"She was run over by a train. It appears she purposely stood in front of it."

At this incredible information, Jeanette bit her lower lip, clenched her eyes shut, tapped a fisted hand against her mouth, and shook her head in seeming disbelief. The detectives feared she might break down as well, but after several, drawn-out moments, she regained her composure.

"Why do you keep saying, 'it appears'? What does that mean? Did she commit suicide or not?" Jeanette demanded answers. There was an edge to her voice now. She glared at Roger Matthews as if he was the one who did something to Renee.

"That's what we are trying to determine for certain," Detective Scott Arnold explained, ending his muteness.

"We're here to ask a few questions and wrap up our investigation of her death. That's all," Roger clarified. "May we please see Renee's office? I was going to ask Ms. Donaldson, but she is still overwrought by the news."

"Of course you can see Renee's office," Jeanette answered for both her and Charly. "But what are you looking for?"

"A suicide note. Her husband hasn't found one at their home," Scott divulged.

Another tremor ran up Jeanette spine. "I'll lead you to her desk," she told the two detectives. As they started away, Jeanette stopped beside Deputy Jordan. "Jack, can you see that Charly gets back to her desk okay?" she asked.

"Of course, Jeannette," he agreed. He looked a bit shell-shocked himself.

"Thanks, Jack," She said and squeezed his arm in gratitude. She swiftly led the detectives away.

Chapter 2

The Note

The detectives made a sweeping appraisal of Renee's office – a small cubicle by the back window. A computer monitor and keyboard sat on one side of the desk. On the right side of the monitor stood a three-by-five picture of Renee and her husband, Mitchell. On the left-hand side stood a much newer, larger photo – five-by-eight – of her infant daughter, Susanna. Push-pinned prayers, funny sayings, cartoons and wallet pictures of other family members – her mom and dad, sister, nieces and nephews – adorned the grey, cloth, modular walls.

On the other side of the desk sat her in-box and several stacks of paper – all organized neatly. The items push-pinned along this wall pertained strictly to business – phone lists, cheat notes for job duties, etc. Roger concentrated his efforts on the stacked paper documents.

He slipped on disposable, rubber gloves before he touched the first item. He bid Scott to do likewise, even though he touched nothing. Scott merely hovered in back of Roger, scrutinizing his every move, like the perfect student.

In the farthest stack over, right on top, in plain sight, laid a white envelope. Roger's eyes caught the name *Mitch* written on the outside, in tiny, flawless penmanship. He picked up the envelope. He could feel something in it. He turned the envelope over and discovered the flap folded inward, but not sealed. He carefully freed the flap and pulled forth a greeting card.

The tagline at the top, over a generic picture of a compass, read: *I'm Sorry…* Inside on the right-hand side was a canned verse: *Sometimes we all lose direction in our lives. I apologize for being so lost lately. Thanks for being there for me.*

On the left-hand side of the card, a brief, personalized note, simple and to the point, read: *Mitch, I love you and Susanna very much. Forgive me. Renee.*

With a grimace, Roger handed the card to his partner. Scott took a second to read it. Then he placed the card in a plastic, sealable bag. He fastened the bag. *Why'd she leave the card here?*, he pondered as he held the evidence.

"What was that? Was it a suicide note?" Jeanette asked. She stood at the opening to Renee's office, monitoring the detectives every move.

"It appears to be. Yes," Roger told her with remorseful eyes. "Can I please get your name and ask you a few more questions?"

"My name is Jeanette O'Riley. I'm the Assistant Jury Manager," she volunteered. "What else do you need to know?"

"I was just wondering. Did Renee seem depressed to you?"

"She…well…Renee was suffering a little from…postpartum depression. Renee's daughter, Susanna, is only three months old. Renee was anxious about the baby. You know, worried about being a good mother. But…suicide?" Jeanette gasped. She turned and stared out the window.

"I think we have all we need here," Roger said. "I'm very sorry about your assistant," he told Jeanette. "Suicide is a terrible thing. It affects so many innocent people."

Jeanette turned and looked at the detectives again, a bewildered look on her face, as if she found it extremely difficult to accept Renee had killed herself. Roger had seen this look many times in his long career as a detective.

"Thank you for all of your help," he said in conclusion.

"Sure," Jeanette said in a quiet, defeated voice.

Roger motioned for Scott to follow him out. Scott thought about relaying his sympathies as well, but thought better of it. Saying he was sorry seemed lame. Plus, he desired to be on his way. He wanted to talk to his partner in private. Some of things with Renee's suicide were not adding up for him, and he wanted to find out if Roger felt the same way.

Chapter 3

Dressing Down

Out on the sidewalk in front of the Jefferson County Judicial Center, Scott decided to break his silence. "So is that it?" Scott gingerly asked his partner.

"Is 'what' it?" Roger asked, sounding a bit irritated. He stepped off to the side a bit so as not to block the doorway.

"Are we going to rule Renee Peterson's death a suicide and be done with it?" Scott questioned. He took a second to absently glance at the pleasing-to-the-eye, spiral columned structure to the front of the Judicial Center. A newer building in downtown Louisville, this design had an age-old, Greek Revival Architecture flare to it. It seemed to tease matching to the old County Courthouse a block over at Sixth and Jefferson. The County Courthouse displayed four, gigantic, sandstone columns in the front of the building.

Roger stepped up to the curb to wait for the traffic light to change. Scott followed, still patiently waiting for his partner's reply to his question. Their office was a short distance away on the opposite side of the street.

They could have chosen to stay inside. A walkway connected the Judicial Center to the Hall of Justice – the building they were facing. From the Hall of Justice, another walkway ran perpendicular into their building – Police

Headquarters. Nice weather called for a walk outside – a breath of fresh air.

They stood right in the heart of the Louisville metropolitan legal justice system. In front of Police Headquarters resided the City Hall annex, and in front of this annex sat the City Hall building, another historical structure, built in a French style, with heavy hood molding around the windows and a tall side-tower, which showcased a white, four-sided, working, Roman numeral clock. The Jefferson County Jail Complex, a modern building, loomed on the other side of the Hall of Justice at Sixth and Liberty.

Noting the bright white WALK sign flashing across the street and that traffic halted, Roger advanced into the intersection. Scott fell into pace beside his partner – a feat none too easy. Six-foot-five, Scott back-pedaled a step for every short step five-foot-six Roger took. Otherwise, he would have been yards ahead.

They passed other men and women in suits and folks in casual clothes. They gave them a glance, and continued on down the street. They strolled – at least it felt like strolling to Scott – up a ramp to the front doors of their building.

Roger finally broke his silence asking, "What else would you have us do but close the case? There is no proof to suggest Renee Peterson's death was anything but suicide."

A detective for many years, he always got stuck training the new guys. Scott seemed to be an improvement over some of the men he had been stuck with, but he was still very green.

"Something doesn't feel right about all this to me," Scott began to justify.

They stepped within the building, coming face-to-face with the Information Booth – a glassed-in structure sitting on a black pedestal base. Roger and Scott veered off to the left.

They stopped to wait on an elevator, heading for their offices on the second floor.

"What doesn't seem right?" Roger asked. "Facts are what tell the story. So let's go over the facts. First...," he began, pointing his index finger in the air for further emphasis.

The elevator arrived. The white doors opened, and they stepped aboard. Roger pushed the *2* button. The doors clinked shut and the elevator lifted. An overwhelming metallic smell lingered in the small enclosed space, so Scott hoped they had a speedy ride.

"First," Roger started again. "Renee's husband Mitchell admits they had a fight."

The elevator reached its destination and the doors opened. Scott stepped out. Roger also vacated the elevator. "Second...Renee's husband told us she was suffering from some bad episodes of postpartum depression," Roger continued.

They faced a glass block enclosure with a door beside it. Roger pressed an intercom button. When the receptionist saw who it was, she pressed the security release button. With a click, the door unlocked.

Scott reached to open the door. The two detectives walked into the area. Directly in front of them, painted on the wall, in big block letters was: *Criminal Investigations Unit*. They turned right and headed down a short hallway toward their office areas. Roger continued his important crusade, "Third...we find a card...from Renee...to her husband...that says she has lost her way and begs his forgiveness."

Scott's office space – a metal desk with a wood look, Formica top – was by the wall. Roger's desk was right beside his. Other desks resided around them – each set of partners' desks side by side, like Roger's and Scott's. Many conversations could be overheard around the room, both between partners and detectives on phones.

Roger approached his desk, pulled out his chair and took a seat. "Fourth...one of Renee's coworkers also admits Renee suffered from postpartum depression. How much more evidence do you need, Scott? Sounds like a pretty clear-cut case of suicide to me. But perhaps we should disregard all the evidence and go with your feeling. Is that what you are suggesting?"

"No...not exactly..." Scott went to his desk and sat down.

"So what's your problem with closing this case?" Roger asked. Rocking back in his seat and tapping his fingers together, he gave Scott a hard stare.

"It's just...well...in case studies of women's suicides, they don't usually choose to die in such a brutal manner. Not only did Renee let a train run over her, but she staked handcuffs to the sides of track and fastened her ankles with them."

Her crushed, severed legs had still been there on the track, with the jumbled handcuffs still fastened around the ankles. "An overdose of pills is the most chosen path for a woman," Scott relayed the facts as he understood them.

"Studies! I should have figured," Roger mocked, shaking his head. *These rookies think they can learn everything they need in some book.* "Well, did your precious 'studies' ever bring you across information on postpartum psychosis? Women do a lot of things out of the ordinary when they are in this state. I was on one case where a mother drowned all of her children. 'Studies' would tell you that this is not 'normal' for a woman either."

"But if Renee was psychotic, wouldn't she have decided to end it all on a quick whim?" Scott questioned. "Instead, she left her car at Walmart, where she caught the bus each day, set off on foot and walked for miles down the railroad track to pick the perfect spot. She had a hammer, handcuffs and anchors with her. It seems she carefully planned each thing. And why were the handcuffs engraved with initials JCJ – not matching Renee or her husband? And why did she leave the suicide note at the office and not at home? My gut tells me something's wrong here."

Stopping the rocking motion of his chair and glaring at Scott, Roger spewed, "You're grasping at straws here, rookie. Psychotic people can, and do, plan gruesome things. As to the engraving on the handcuffs, who knows…she may have bought them at a pawn shop for all we know. It's irrelevant where she obtained the handcuffs. As to the suicide note being left at the office, doing this makes perfect sense to me. If she left it at home, and hubby found it before she did the deed, he might have been able to stop her. Leaving it at the office makes sure he…or someone…finds it after the fact."

"I guess that all makes sense," Scott begrudgingly agreed.

"You're damn right it does!" Roger proclaimed. Then he added in a stern voice, "Perhaps I should make something very clear to you, Scott. I was investigating murders before you were born. I know a few more things, from valuable experience, then you will ever be able to learn from a million books. So if we go with anyone's gut feeling here, it will be mine. And my gut, unlike yours, says this lady killed herself. Now, unless you can give me some *hard* evidence to refute my gut, then this case is closed. Have you got that?"

"Yes, sir," he reluctantly agreed. As Roger pointed out, he had too many years of hands-on experience over him. *I'm the new guy on the block, so I have to bow to Roger's final assessment of Renee's death.*

"Let it go, rookie," Roger demanded, noting Scott's continued pensiveness. "We'll have many more important cases for you to obsess over."

"Yeah, I'm sure," Scott conceded. *Roger has the expertise. He has to be right,* he tried to convince himself. But a nagging doubt remained in the back of his mind.

He listened as Roger picked up the phone and called Commonwealth Attorney, Darrell Adams, to inform him the case had been ruled a suicide.

* * * *

"How nuts," Darrell replied, upon hearing Roger's assessment of Renee Peterson's death. "Well, I guess at least the lady is better off than Mary."

"How's your sister doing?" Roger asked. He had known Darrell over fifteen years. His younger sister Mary laid in a coma at a psychiatric hospital. A date rape in college had left her mentally disturbed. A failed suicide attempt had catapulted her into her latest grime situation.

"As well as can be expected. They don't expect she will ever come out of a coma," Darrell revealed, his vocal tone solemn.

"I hate to hear that," Roger replied in an equally somber voice. "My prayers are with you and your sister, buddy."

"I know. Thanks," Darrell responded. "I'll let you get back to your paperwork. I'm sure there is plenty for you to fill out to close the Renee Peterson case. Thanks for letting me know what you guys found."

"You betcha. Talk to you later," Roger said, and lowered the phone receiver. *Poor Darrell,* he thought as he got up from his desk and went to get a cup of coffee and get on with his morning. Glad they were putting the Renee Peterson case to bed, he'd finish the paperwork on this death and move on to more important matters. Many cases – more pressing – needed his attention.

* * * *

Later that evening, the opportunity arose for Scott to share his doubts about Renee's death with another person – his girlfriend, Debbie Gray. Dating about six months now, they met at Phoenix Hill one night after Scott had been talked into going to this local nightclub by some buddies. Scott had spied Debbie there with some of her girlfriends. Later that night, Scott convinced Debbie to share a slow dance with him, and he had bought her a drink. They began to talk, and twenty-six-year-old Scott and twenty-five-year-old Debbie hit it off right away.

Debbie worked for CASA – Court Appointed Special Advocates for children. She acted on behalf of kids involved in Family Court. With a kind and giving heart, Debbie seemed an ideal person for this position. Scott was smitten almost from the start. Of course, Debbie's attractive body, long, shimmering black hair, and big, beautiful, bright green eyes did not escape his attention either.

This evening, Debbie invited him over for dinner at her house. Debbie lived in a two-bedroom, brick house in Shively, in the south end of Louisville. Seated at a small wooden table in the kitchen, Debbie noticed Scott was more quiet than usual. "Is everything okay?" she asked.

He finished chewing up the bite of lasagna he had in his mouth. Then, in his preoccupation, with exaggerated enthusiasm, he answered, "Oh, your lasagna is to die for!"

"I didn't mean the food," she chuckled, laying down her fork and reaching to caress his hand. "I meant with you. You seem like something's bothering you."

"It is," he admitted, chewing up another bite of his food. Whatever was bothering him did not seem to be hindering his appetite. Because of his height, Scott could eat and eat and scarcely gain a pound. "I investigated my first homicide today as a detective."

"Oh…was it bad?" she asked.

The concerned, focused look on Debbie's face touched Scott's heart. *She is so caring.* He loved this quality in her. He also found her hair, immaculately swept up off her neck and styled in a roll on the back of her head, very attractive, as usual. Both still dressed from their jobs downtown, Debbie donned a green sweater and black slacks, and Scott wore a navy suit, although he had removed his tie.

"It was bad," Scott confessed. "A lady was handcuffed to a train track and got hit by a train."

"Oh!" Debbie gasped, gritting her teeth and shaking her head. Her mind conjured a horrifying image. "I can only…and only want to…imagine…what you saw. I'm sorry, Scott."

"It was a little gruesome, but it's my job," he replied. He bent to give Debbie a grateful kiss. "What bothers me is her death has been ruled a suicide."

"And you don't think it was?" Debbie questioned. She had to shake the lingering image of this poor woman's death before she could continue eating.

"The bulk of the evidence seems to say it was suicide. Her husband and a co-worker said she was suffering from postpartum depression, and we found what we think was a suicide note. But…"

"But it's hard to imagine someone committing suicide that way," Debbie finished his sentence.

"Exactly. Especially a woman. She seemed to put a lot of planning into this 'suicide'. But our job is to collect evidence, and we rule on what the evidence tells us, and my boss has deemed this evidence screamed 'suicide', so that's it."

"You said she had postpartum depression. So this woman had children?"

"Yes. A three-month old daughter."

"Oh...how horrible," Debbie wailed. She looked troubled now.

"I'm sorry," Scott apologized. "I shouldn't be discussing such gloomy things."

"You should if it's on your mind," Debbie argued. "I love you, Scott. We share the good and the bad."

"I love you too, Debbie," he said. He took a drink of tea to wash down some more lasagna.

Glad to have someone to share things with, he bent to bestow a lingering kiss on her full, ruby lips. As soon as he saved a little more money, he planned to buy an engagement ring and propose to this special lady. He looked forward to spending the rest of his life with her.

Scott purposely changed the subject, telling Debbie about something funny that had happened that day. She laughed, and he enjoyed seeing her smile again. They settled into a relaxing evening together, happy to be in one another's company.

Chapter 4

Reminiscing

A tingle ran up his spine as he heard it announced on the news: "In the early morning hours, a woman was struck and killed by a train near the Valley Station area. Investigators have ruled that Renee Peterson, twenty-six, a resident of the Valley Station area, committed suicide when she purposely stood on the track in front of a train. Her husband and a co-worker told investigators Renee was suffering from postpartum depression. She leaves behind a husband and a three-month-old daughter." The reporter moved on to the next story, scarcely taking a breath in-between.

Not interested in the other news, he picked up the remote and muted the sound. He also took a seat on the couch; his legs trembled. *I've done it!* he concluded with a rush of euphoria. *I can have it all now. I can move on with my life since Renee has been eliminated.*

He replayed every detail of Renee's murder in his mind's eye, over and over, since that morning. He should be disgusted. He should feel overwhelming guilt. But instead, he experienced a joyful upsurge every time he relived his part in Renee's death.

He laid his head back on the top of the sofa, closed his eyes, and prepared to relish it all again. He almost laughed when he thought about how she could have easily messed up his plans. If she had resisted and forced him to shoot her, then it would *not* have looked like suicide. But Renee had not resisted – not in any way. Renee obeyed like a meek little lamb – a lamb he took to the slaughter. He did laugh as he thought of this intoxicating correlation.

"Where are we going?" she had asked, as they headed farther and farther down Dixie Highway. They went to dinner right after work, and then to karaoke for hours. It had been almost midnight.

"One last stop and then you'll be home," he said with a conniving smile.

"We should go home now. We both have to be up early tomorrow to go to work. Susanna is at my mom's, so at least I don't have to worry about her."

"No, you don't have to worry about Susanna," he assured her, sounding a bit strange. He continued to drive.

When he pulled the car off the beaten path, into a wooded area, and stopped, Renee sounded worried, "What's wrong? Why are we stopping here?" she questioned.

He did not answer. He merely got out of his car, went around back, and opened the trunk. He pulled out Renee's purse and a hammer – the hammer he had initially laid on the front seat. Renee had picked it up when she first got into the car, several hours ago. "What's this?" she had asked.

"Oh, I'll just put that in the trunk," he had answered. He had hit the trunk release button, took the hammer from her hand, got out of the car, and put the hammer in the trunk. Naturally, he had on gloves, but Renee had not. It was November, so gloves did not seem all that strange, even though it was a rather mild evening.

Now, as he retrieved Renee's purse and the hammer from the trunk, he unzipped her purse and stuck the hammer inside. He zipped the purse back up with the handle of the hammer sticking out. He also retrieved a flashlight.

He heard the passenger door open. As he shut the trunk, he saw Renee get out of the car. *Perfect!*

"What are you doing?" she asked as she approached him.

He pulled a gun on her. The bewildered expression on her face made his day. She trusted him, so this turn of events came as quite a shock.

"Let's go for a little walk," he ordered, turning on the flashlight.

"Where are you taking me?" she asked. Looking into the dark, dense woods on the other side of them, terror showed on her face.

"That's for me to know and you to find out," he said with a devious chuckle. "Now let's move," he instructed, swinging the gun a little closer.

When they entered the woods, and began to walk alongside a railroad track, the real excitement started to build. If he was going to have second thoughts about what he was doing, it would have been then. But there were no second thoughts.

"Why are you doing this?" she questioned.

"Why? There are too many reasons. Most of all because you don't appreciate what you've got…the perfect life…a loving husband and a precious daughter…"

"But I do! I've just been depressed. You know that," Renee argued in a pitiful, whiny voice. The grating sound of her voice made him want to do away with her even more.

"Step up on the track," he ordered when they got to the right spot. His flashlight picked up a gleam from the metal on the handcuffs.

He had shed some nervous perspiration when he had prepared this spot for Renee's impending demise, just before dawn. It was fall; the trees were bare, but still a small forest on both sides obstructed a clear view of the railroad track. There also were no homes close by.

Regardless, at one point, while he hammered in the steel talon anchors, which held the handcuffs firm to the track, he heard a dog bark. He froze for fear of discovery. But he soon determined the dog was not close and did not seem to be moving in his direction, so he quickly finished the task at hand.

Now, just after midnight, his plan commenced flawlessly, better than planned. A card in Renee's purse – the purse he now carried – a note of apology – could be construed as a suicide note. Tickled by this turn of events, he planned to take the note out of her purse and leave the card on her desk at work. Everything seemed to be coming together superbly.

"Snap the handcuffs around your ankles," he ordered, his last request of her. He would leave, go hide in the woods, watch, and wait. His heart raced in frenzied anticipation.

He heard her call *the name he was known by* in a pleading manner. "Do as I ask!" he commanded through gritted teeth, chambering the bullet, and aiming the gun toward Renee's head. "Or I'll splatter your brain all over the track."

"You're ill," Renee said in a trembling voice. Tears ran down her checks; her hands shook. She bent on wobbly legs. With unsure hands, she hooked one handcuff around each ankle and snapped them shut. They locked. He could tell by the sound.

"You can get help. You need to stop all this. You're a good person. You don't want to hurt me. What about Susanna? You don't want to take her mother away from her," Renee beseeched him.

"I'm doing this *for* Susanna," he told her with an evil grin.

As he turned and hurried away, he retrieved the valued card from her purse. Then he tossed the purse in the grass just out of her reach. Renee screamed his name over and over again. He ignored her.

No one around, he did not care if she screamed her head off. He concealed himself in the woods, turned off his flashlight, and waited with baited breath. *It shouldn't be long now. The train goes through here every morning at 12:20.* Planning Renee's murder for some time, he had done his research. Now that he executed his plan, he struggled to believe the reality.

Renee struggled like a trapped animal. She pulled and jerked at the handcuffs with all her strength. She kicked at the anchors over and over, trying to dislodge their hold. As she thrashed about, she cut and bruised herself. He wondered for a moment if she would attempt to bite her feet off, like a wild animal.

In a sick moment, he wished he provided her the means to free herself – perhaps a hatchet. Then, after she cut off her own feet, he could have shot her as she struggled to try and pull herself away. *But no! Being run over by a train will look like suicide. It's the perfect crime.*

Renee cried and shrieked some more. Hoarse and fatigued, she eventually collapsed on the track, defeated. She dropped her head in her hands, and she wailed and wailed.

She's giving up, he concluded with delight.

However, when she heard the train approaching, she stood back up. He heard her scream his name again – one last fleeting hope he would have mercy, spring forth, and release her.

Sorry, little Renee, but it isn't going to happen, he resolved heartlessly. His thirst for blood too great, Renee's death loomed.

In the last few moments, as the train got closer and closer, Renee's terror hung like dense fog in the air. It gave him a surge of adrenaline. *This is better than sex could ever be.*

He could not believe she stood back up. This beat anything he could have imagined. The coupling on the front of the engine stabbed into the lower half of her; her legs ripped from her body.

He anticipated her flattened and mangled by the train. Instead, the top half of Renee's body flew from the track and slammed hard into a tree. It all happened in an instant. Power coursed through him. He discovered something magnificent that morning. *It is good to kill!*

Chapter 5

Sympathy

At 4:55 p.m., Mitch opened the glass door to the Jury Administrator's office and approached a wood topped, grey counter. He visited this office to collect his wife's personal belongings. The counter out front enabled the jury administrators to greet potential jurors and talk with them.

A dentist's appointment left Charly's cubicle empty, but Jeanette sat at her desk. Mitch looked over the counter, past a printer station, and into her low wall cubicle. A wall with a picture on it stood behind her partition. A bookcase enclosed the back of Charly's office – another low wall cubicle to the right. The low wall cubicle behind the bookcase, back by the window, had belonged to Renee.

Glad to see Mitchell again, Jeanette smiled at him as she left her office space. She approached the counter. Mitchell's lips curved in response. A tall man, with short, wavy, black hair, a full, nicely groomed mustache and beard, and engaging, deep dark brown eyes, Mitchell captivated the female eye. His arresting good looks aside, he also worked out at a gym on a regular basis to add ample muscles to his chest, arms and legs.

A Chief Investment Officer for PNC Bank, no appointments filled his schedule today, so a casual wardrobe prevailed – tan slacks and a red polo shirt. The red shirt made his eyes stand out even more.

Jeanette talked to Mitchell at length at the funeral home, and she lent her comfort once more at Renee's funeral. Mitch gave her a tight, grateful hug each time. Jeanette liked the way his arms felt around her, like a warm, secure blanket. She also liked his smell – Armani Black. She knew what cologne Mitchell wore because she had shopped with Renee when she bought it for him, for his birthday.

As Jeanette stood at the counter, less than a foot away from him, she could not help but notice this alluring fragrance once more. Jeanette secretly harbored a crush on Mitchell. *But it's much too soon to be thinking anything like that. Mitch needs friends and support. There is no way he's thinking of moving on romantically this soon.* Renee had only been dead a week.

"I bet you are here for Renee's things," she assumed. Jeanette placed her hands on top of the counter and leaned toward him a little more. Her brilliant blue eyes sparkled. Her curly, short, red hair seemed to be a natural compliment to her blue eyes. It made them even more compelling.

"Yeah. I am," Mitch admitted. His lips straight lined and his voice sounded somber.

"I'll open the door for you, so you can go back to Renee's office. I can go to the copy room and get you some empty, copy paper boxes if you like. They are nice for moving stuff. Would you like some help, or do you want to be left alone."

"Help would be great. Company would be even better," he said. A slight smile appeared on his face as he stole an unsubtle glance at her ample cleavage. Her large breasts, revealing blouse, and lean toward him made it virtually impossible to miss. Not that he wanted to miss this mouthwatering view.

"Okay. I can give you both, help and company," Jeanette said, returning his smile. She disappeared around the corner. Jeanette unlocked a door to the right, up by the front glass. She motioned for Mitch to enter.

Mitch walked through the doorway. Standing right beside Jeanette now, he made casual conversation, as they walked off together toward Renee's office space. "So how is it going, Jeanette?"

"Okay. We still miss Renee. We'll have to hire another assistant, but neither Charly nor I are in the frame of mind to do so right now. How are you and Susanna doing?" They walked toward the window, strolling past Charly's office.

"Susanna and I are doing alright," he answered, sounding a little downtrodden. "Renee's absence isn't affecting Susanna much. With Renee suffering from postpartum, she was barely interacting with the baby. So Susanna didn't have much to miss."

Jeanette noted bitterness in Mitch's voice. "It had to be hard on you dealing with Renee's depression and a new baby." Jeanette spoke thoughts she had entertained for some time. Renee had disclosed that she did not want to be around her own baby and her marriage with Mitch suffered as well.

"It was hard," Mitch admitted with a frown.

They stepped into the opening on the side of Renee's cubicle. Nothing looked disturbed. It still appeared as if Renee would be coming back. This state of affairs shook Mitch a bit.

"Are you okay?" Jeanette asked, touching his arm. Distress showed in his striking, brown eyes.

"I will be. Would you mind getting me those boxes?"

"Of course not. I'll be right back," Jeanette said. She gave his arm another reassuring squeeze, noting the muscle in it, before she hurried away.

Mitch made his way over to Renee's desk. He picked up the picture of Susanna first. Then he fingered the one of him and Renee. *It looks like she had such a perfect little family life. Instead it was all such a sham,* he contemplated with torment.

He stacked the framed pictures – facedown. Next, he pulled down the pictures push pinned to the walls. He placed them facedown on top of the other pictures. He could not bear to look at any of these items. *It's all such a lie. Renee didn't care about anyone. She was lost in her own dark, disturbed world.*

Jeanette appeared at the entranceway to the cubicle again a few moments later. She sat one empty box on the floor outside the cubicle. She discarded the lid from the other and sat the box on the corner of Renee's desk. She reached to pick up the items Mitchell moved, and she placed them in the container. "One box may be enough."

"It probably will be," he mumbled. He opened a drawer and examined its contents. "I hate this," he mumbled. His head bent, he looked as if he bore the weight of the world on his broad shoulders.

"I know. It's got to be hard…"

"It is hard. It's hard because…oh, never mind," he said, shaking his head

"What, Mitch? What is it?" Jeanette questioned with concern, addressing him by his shortened name, as Renee always had. For a second time, she squeezed his lower arm with her hand. *He has nice muscles.*

"I'm angry, Jeanette," he confessed. He took some of his frustration out on the drawer, slamming it shut. He jerked open another drawer instead. "I know Renee was ill, but it's been hell living with her since Susanna was born. You expect your wife to have an instant bond with your children, but she wanted nothing to do with Susanna. And she wanted even less to do with me. Many nights I would have a crying baby in one room and a crying wife in the other. Frankly, in some ways, as terrible as it sounds, I'm glad it's all ended."

Jeanette looked shocked by Mitch's harsh words. She never knew he felt this way. But she could sympathize with his sentiments. Living with Renee, and her postpartum depression, spelled household chaos.

"I'm sorry. I shouldn't be unloading on you," Mitch apologized. He tossed some more odds and ins – an old Employee of the Quarter Certificate, some gum, candy bars and a few small bags of pretzels – into the box. Then he slid this drawer closed with a bang. He moved right on to the next drawer, jerking it open.

"It's okay if you unload on me, Mitch. You sound as if you need an ear. Would you like to talk some more? We could go to dinner after you're through here if you like."

At the mention of dinner, he looked down at his wristwatch. "Am I...I'm holding you up, aren't I? It's after five. Your workday is through..."

"It is through. So I'm free to lend you an ear. So what about dinner?" Jeanette persisted. She wanted to spend some more time with Mitchell. She wanted to be there for him.

"It sounds good," he agreed, giving her a grateful smile. "Thanks, Jeanette. You're a sweet lady." *Not to mention a very pretty one.* Suddenly looking very forward to dinner, Mitch took a fleeting look at her ample bust line once more.

Chapter 6

Deputy Jack

Jack reached back and fingered his new handcuffs, the second pair he replaced. It would not have looked right for a deputy sheriff to walk around without his handcuffs. Each day Jack's uniform consisted of a crisp, clean, brown shirt with his gleaming badge on the left side, his polished name tag on the right, a gold JCS pin on his collar, and triangular patches denoting Jefferson County Sheriff's Department at the top of each sleeve. A brown stripe, running down the side of each pant leg, set off his tan, wrinkle free pants. His black gun belt, socks and shoes added a nice contrast to the rest of his uniform.

Jack, a deputy sheriff for years, also earned the right to display five gold stripes on the arm of his shirt sleeve. Each gold stripe represented five years of service. Jack had been a deputy sheriff for almost thirty years. If he stayed around a few more years, he would earn his sixth stripe. But Jack had begun to contemplate retiring.

After all, the sheriff's department, in effect, had put him out to pasture – working at the Judicial Center. Most of his days entailed watching people walk through metal detectors as they entered the building, and walking potential jurors to courtrooms. Occasionally, he got lucky and got to escort some pretty lady to her car at the close of the evening – his biggest excitement.

Disconcerting as well, his wife of many years had divorced him six months ago. His wife claimed some nonsense about them living an emotional divorce – *some crap she learned from watching the Dr. Phil Show*, he ascertained.

Still bitter about their breakup, Jack believed he gave his ex-wife a good life. Not able to have children, they had lived in a nice house together – the house *she* still lived in; a slick attorney arranged this provision in their divorce agreement. He had always provided his wife with a decent car to drive – she took one of these with her as well. He might not have gone on and on about how he felt, but he was a man; he was not supposed to bather on about his emotions. But his wife had not seen it this way. Everything he gave her was not good enough. She had not appreciated anything. He hated her now.

* * * *

Jack approached Jeanette, sitting at a table for two, by the wall, in the dining hall in the Hall of Justice. A half-eaten ham and cheese sandwich, a bag of opened chips, and a Pepsi sat in front of her. Reading a paperback novel, she did not see Jack draw near.

He pulled out the chair across from her and took a seat. The motion and noise of the chair captured Jeanette's attention. When she saw Jack sit down, she picked up a bookmark and placed it in the book. Then she sat the book on the table beside her lunch.

"Hi, Jack," she greeted. Her face revealed no sign of happiness to see him. If anything, she seemed aggravated by his presence.

Jack was irritated by Jeanette's nonchalance. "So how are you, Jeanette? You haven't returned any of my calls. I saw you meet Renee's husband – or should I say, her widower – out front. Is he the reason for your unexplained dismissal?"

"Jack," she said, her voice barely above a whisper. "What you and I had was nice. But it was *not* some big romance. You need to accept that."

"So what was I…some sort of short diversion for you?"

"Jack, this isn't the time, or the place, to talk about this," she told him, glancing about. It was 12:30 – prime lunchtime – so the dining area was packed. She did not want this conversation overheard by colleagues. "Can we meet for a drink after work?"

"Just a drink?" he asked with a longing insinuation.

"Yes. *Just* a drink," Renee stressed.

"You know. All of you women are just alike," he snapped, throwing his chair back and leaping to his feet. His eyes looked daggers at her now. His crimson face, in combination with his orange hair, made his head almost look like a flame. His blue eyes were even more pronounced. "You take what you want from a man and then you toss them aside. You better learn to appreciate when things are good, or you will be sorry some day."

Jeanette recoiled at Jack's outburst. Out of character for him, he usually came across so serene. She noticed, with embarrassment, many heads turned to look in their direction. She *was* sorry about their brief affair.

"Jack, please…" she pleaded.

"You're disgusting, Jeanette. You know that," he spat as he dashed away.

Jack was angry with everyone. None of them appreciated what they had. *Renee had not appreciated what she had. She had been blessed with a beautiful baby girl, but she acted as if she did not want her. Jeanette found a good man in him, but she did not appreciate this fact. Renee's husband obviously had not appreciated her, or he would not already be moving on with a whore – Jeanette.* Jack hated everyone. *They all deserve to burn in hell,* he fumed as he trudged off in a huff.

Chapter 7

The Proposal

Only the second time they had been out together, Jeanette and Mitch shared a heated kiss in a bar. Now, they headed back to his house in his Toyota Accord. Renee had not been dead two weeks, and Mitch was ready, willing, and able to move on.

Should I be doing this? Jeanette second-guessed her actions.

Mitch must have sensed her uncertainty, because he began reassuring her, "It's okay, Jeanette. What you have to realize is Renee and I had not been together sexually in a very long time. I know she hasn't been dead long, but our marriage started to die a long time ago. So don't feel guilty, okay?"

"It's just a little strange, that's all," she confessed. It was *very* strange for her. She entertained fantasies of what it would be like to be with Mitchell, from the first time she saw him at an office Christmas party with Renee. Now, her dream about to come to fruition, she wondered if her other dreams, of having a perfect little family with Mitch, would also come true. She would soon find out. She yearned to get to his house.

* * * *

Things progressed at the speed of sound between Jeanette and Mitchell after that first night. Her dreams seemed to be coming true. Spending more and more nights at his place, she bonded with Susanna as well.

I can't believe Renee did not want to be a mother to this precious little girl. Jeanette thought as she rocked the baby to sleep one night. A very agreeable baby, Susanna only cried when hungry or needing a diaper change, and even then she gave a simple whimper instead of a loud bellow.

Mitch stood in the doorway to his daughter's nursery. A small, angel nightlight provided the only illumination in the room. He spent many a night rocking Susanna to sleep in this very room. He also spent many hours decorating this room before his baby girl was born.

Since Renee had not wanted to know the sex of the baby, he painted the room a pale yellow. In contrast, he applied a wallpaper border of white sheep, and green, blue and yellow bears up close to the ceiling. A changing table and diaper pail stood on one side of the room. Susanna's walnut crib, with a colorful, rotating, musical mobile overhead had been placed against the other wall. A honey-colored, rubber-wood, rocking chair had its place beside the crib. Under the window, a bright green and blue, heavy plastic, Fisher Price toy box sat, with a giant, white, stuffed bear on top.

Mitch smiled as he watched Jeanette rock his daughter. "You know, you are a natural at that," he commented in a soft voice. "It's good to know Susanna has someone in her life who will love and appreciate her now." *I'm glad Renee is out of our lives*, he thought, but did not dare utter.

"Renee was sick. That's all there is to it. I can see that more and more as I spend time with Susanna. She's a darling."

"Yes, she is," he agreed and walked over to the rocking chair. He bent and gave Jeanette a warm kiss on the lips. "And so are you. I think Susanna could use a brother or a sister some day. How do you think that would be?"

The happy expression on Jeanette's face at once turned to a grimace. "Is that what you are looking for? A woman who can pop out more kids for you?"

Mitch found this statement strange, and he puzzled at the anger in Jeanette's voice. "Not necessarily," he answered. "What I was trying to say is I think you would make an excellent mother, both to Susanna and to any other kids we might have. I'm falling in love with you, Jeanette. I know it's soon. But it's how I feel."

Conflicting emotions filled Jeanette – joy to hear Mitch say he loved her and fear at his mention of having more children. She looked down into Susanna's tiny, flawless, adorable face. Pleased to discover she had fallen asleep, she carefully stood and bent over the baby's crib. She tenderly laid Susanna on her back and covered her tiny body to the neck with a soft pink, baby blanket.

"Can we go in the den and talk?" she asked Mitch in a soft voice.

"Of course. I think we should," he agreed, anxious to find out if Jeanette had feelings for him as well. She cared a great deal about Susanna.

They walked down the hallway and into the den. The den also doubled as Mitchell's home office. The room contained a loveseat, a nineteen-inch television, and a stereo. Adding to the office element, Mitchell's framed BA certificate hung on a far wall over a desk with a computer on it. On the opposite wall, some baby pictures of Susanna hung. No pictures whatsoever of Renee sat on tables or adorned walls. Jeanette could not help but wonder if there never had been any or if Mitch did away with them all. He had erased all sign of

Renee from his life already. She found this situation eerie, but gratifying.

They took a seat, side by side, on the loveseat. Mitch placed his arm around her shoulder. "So did I spook you in there? Am I coming on too strong too soon?" he asked. His handsome, dark brown eyes fixed with her bright blue ones. He also reached to finger a curl from her short auburn hair.

"No and yes," Jeanette answered. She reached to stroke his beard as she added, "I have feelings for you too, Mitch. In fact, I think I might be falling in love with you as well..."

"That's wonderful!" He gushed and gave her a quick kiss.

"But...you may not want me..."

"Why would I not want you? You're wonderful! You're a fantastic lover...full of imagination. You certainly know how to pleasure a man," he professed with dancing eyes. He also added, "And as I said, you'll make a terrific mother. What's not to want?"

"You mentioned having other children..." She stopped touching him and skittishly looked down into her lap.

"I wasn't talking about having children right away. I was talking down the road," Mitch tried to ease her concern.

"It doesn't matter if it's right away or down the road," Jeanette revealed. Like a shy child, she peeked upward into his eyes again. With a sick feeling in the pit of her stomach, she confessed, "I can't have children, Mitch. I...I'm barren."

"Are you certain?" he asked. As he noted the sadness in her eyes, he realized he asked a dumb question.

"I don't have ovaries or a womb. So, yes, I am quite certain," Jeanette snapped. Her lips stretched in a tight, irate line.

"I'm sorry," Mitch empathized. "You're only thirty-two. I wouldn't have figured something like that..."

"So…now that you know, is this the end for us? Are you looking for a whole woman?"

"What? No…of course it isn't the end for us. And you *are* a whole woman. Even if you can't bear children," he stressed, giving her another brief kiss. "It would be nice to have children with you. I think any man wants that with the woman he loves. But I have Susanna. We can raise her together. She'll be like your natural child. You already love her more than her mother did. I can see that. I can live without having other children."

"Are you sure?" Jeanette questioned.

"Positive. I just want you. I'm sorry I brought up a painful issue, but I'm glad I found out about this. Let's move forward from here."

"Move forward how?" she asked. It sounded as if he was proposing. Jeanette's insides stirred. *Could this be possible?* She might finally have a normal life. The picture perfect life she imagined.

"I want us to be a family, Jeanette. I want you to become my wife. I know Renee's only been dead a month, but I'm ready to move on. I've wasted too much time already. So what do you say? Will you marry me?"

She could not believe her ears. Overwhelmed, her breath caught in her throat. *Should I do this? Why shouldn't I? It's what I've always wanted. To hell with what everyone else thinks. I'm moving on with my life. I've made wise decisions to get me to this point. It's time I had what I deserve in life.*

"Jeanette?" Mitch called in a questioning tone, staring into her eyes with anxiousness.

"I can't believe this is happening. Yes, Mitch. Yes! I'll marry you. I'd be proud and happy to both be your wife and Susanna's mom."

"I'm the happiest man alive!" he proclaimed, smothering her with kisses. "Thanks for bringing joy back into my life, Jeanette. You won't regret it."

No, I won't, she decided. It felt great to have a normal life to look forward to.

Chapter 8

Reactions

Mitch and Jeanette eloped on Monday of the next week. Jeanette left a message at the office for Charly on Sunday evening. She still had a week's vacation left to take. She had planned to take it at the end of the year, closer to Christmas, but she told Charly she changed her mind and intended to take her vacation in the coming week instead. She apologized for the short notice, but told her she needed to take this time.

Charly thought the short notice strange, but since Jeanette had the time coming, she did not mind her taking her vacation at this time. They were interviewing applicants to take Renee's place. *Perhaps Jeanette is taking vacation to avoid hiring anyone new. She might be having a difficult time hiring a replacement for Renee. That's okay. I can do it*, Charly decided. When Jeanette returned, there would be a new woman working in Renee's office.

Mitch did not tell anyone what he was doing either. In fact, he lied and told them at work that he needed a week off to track a prospective new client. Since he remained a top sales producer at PNC, the bank appreciated having him take the time off to chase more business.

Mitch also told Renee's parents he needed to leave town on business. They delighted at taking Susanna for a week. Had they had an inkling of what their former son-in-law was up to, they would not have been so thrilled to watch Susanna for him.

Mitch and Jeanette drove to Gatlinburg, Tennessee. They got married by a Justice of the Peace in one of the wedding chapels there. Then they drove up to a cabin in the mountains to spend the rest of their honeymoon in peaceful bliss.

Jeanette relaxed in the Jacuzzi and in front of the fire roaring in the stone fireplace. She enjoyed having Mitch wait on her every need. She amply rewarded him in the king-sized bed.

A little surprised by the frequency of Mitch's needs – several times a day – Jeanette figured this behavior typical for two people on their honeymoon. Overjoyed to have a normal life at last, she conspired, *When we get back home and settle into family life with Susanna, I'll be able to put him off some.*

Jeanette did not get a lot of pleasure from sex. She never had. But it was an art she perfected to please the men in her life. And she wanted to please Mitchell. So, for now, she submitted to his every need.

* * * *

When they returned from their glorious time away, they revealed their secret to everyone. "I want to let my former in-laws know Susanna has a wonderful new step mom," Mitch told Jeanette as they pulled into his in-laws' driveway.

Jeanette suggested he drop her off at his house – her new home – before he picked up Susanna. But Mitch would have no part of this scheme. Being bullheaded, he proclaimed, "No. It's time we start being honest. I don't want to hide our marriage. I want to shout it from the rooftops and let everyone know. They should all be happy for us. If they aren't, that's just tough."

Jeanette suggested she at least wait in the car until after Mitch broke the news, but Mitch would have no part of this plan either. He ushered her from the car, and the two walked side by side up to the door. Mitch rang the doorbell, and Jeanette held her breath.

Marvin, Renee's father, answered the door. A decent sized man, he looked to weigh over 200 pounds. His bald, shiny head looked like a cue ball. Marvin smiled at Mitch, until he glimpsed his arm around Jeanette's waist. Then the smile transformed to an ugly sneer.

"Marvin, I'd like for you to meet Jeanette. Jeanette and I got married a week ago. She is Susanna's new mom." Mitch callously broke the news.

"The hell she is!" Marvin exclaimed. His black eyes narrowed and shot flames at Jeanette. "I don't know who this little hussy is, but she took advantage of your grief, Mitch. Renee's barely been dead a month. You must be out of your mind to have remarried this soon! Besides, Susanna already has a mom. Renee will *always* be Susanna's mom."

"Maybe I better go wait in the car," Jeanette proposed, peeking back at the car – her safe haven.

"A cat would have been a better mother to Susanna than Renee," Mitch proclaimed with malice. He tightened his grip on Jeanette's waist.

"Don't you even think about standing there badmouthing my daughter," Marvin warned, his hands balling into fists.

Jeanette anxiously glanced at Mitch. She bet Marvin's large hands could pack quite a wallop. "I can go wait in the car," she offered in a whisper.

"You will not," Mitch refused a final time. "Marvin, I know you'd like to have a relationship with your granddaughter, so you will have to accept that Jeanette *is* my wife, and Susanna's step mom. I will not have you disrespect her. You're the one who needs to watch his mouth."

"Don't you stand here on my porch step and threaten me, boy!" Marvin warned, taking a step forward. Jeanette's heart began to race. A fight between these two men seemed imminent now.

"Marvin, what's the matter?" Thelma, Renee's mother, asked, as she came from around the corner, holding Susanna in her arms. Short, a bit on the heavy side, with gray hair, which she tucked up into a bun on the back of her head, Thelma looked the perfect image of a grandmother.

"This nitwit has lost his mind. He's gone and remarried already!" Marvin shouted. "Our daughter is barely cold, and he's replaced her. No wonder Renee committed suicide."

This last comment took things too far for Mitch. Mitch's temper flared, and he sent a fist flying in Marvin's direction. It struck Marvin hard in the cheek. He never saw what hit him. He went sprawling back in the floor, narrowly avoiding a collision with his wife. The back of his head struck the marble tile, and Marvin was out like a light.

Thelma screamed, and Susanna began to wail. Mitch charged past Marvin's horizontal body. "Thelma, give me my daughter," he demanded.

Jeanette remained on the porch, with her mouth standing open. She could not believe things turned violent between Mitch and Renee's father.

"Mitch, you need to calm down. You don't want to hurt the baby," Thelma pleaded with him. Her voice quivered, as she looked from the baby's crying face to her unconscious husband.

"I would never hurt Susanna," he professed, pulling her from Thelma's arms. He walked back over to Jeanette and handed her the baby. "Go put her in the car seat," he instructed.

Jeanette turned and headed toward the car. She gently bounced Susanna, trying to alleviate her trauma. A few seconds later, Mitch came from the house carrying Susanna's diaper bag and her tiny suitcase.

"Who needs them!" he growled as he got into the car. He slammed his door, started the car, slammed it in reverse, and raced away.

Jeanette did not say a word. Stupefied by Mitch's violent streak, she hoped he never applied it to their relationship. She would not stand for it if he did. As Susanna began to cry again, Jeanette turned and tried to comfort the baby. But the violent episode between Mitch and his father-in-law kept playing in her mind.

* * * *

Not only did Renee's parents disapprove of Jeanette and Mitch's nuptials, Charly added her negative remarks. "I thought you and Renee were friends," she commented. She stared, in amazement, at Jeanette's large diamond ring and wedding band.

"We were. What's your point?" Jeanette asked. She frowned at Charly.

"My point is...how can you marry Renee's husband when you were her friend?" she bluntly questioned.

"He ceased being Renee's husband when Renee died. Don't you think Renee would want Mitch to be happy?" Jeanette countered.

"I'm sure she would. But I would think Mitch would grieve her for awhile before he moved on to someone else," Charly pointed out. *Moving on this soon is so cold.*

"Well, that's your opinion. I see no reason he needs to wallow in grief for an extended period of time. Renee was sick.

She wanted nothing to do with Mitch or her precious daughter..."

"Precisely...she was sick. Isn't that part of the wedding vows...in sickness and in health? Sounds like Mitch forgot that part."

"You don't know anything about it!" Jeanette retorted. Her eyes glared at Charly; her mouth formed a rigid line. "If you can't be happy for me...for *us*...then we need to drop the subject."

"I think we should," Charly replied. "Would you like to go and meet Renee's replacement? I thought you went on vacation because you couldn't face replacing Renee. What a laugh that was."

"Charly, I'm warning you," Jeanette snarled. *Who's this bitch think she is anyway? Just because she is frigid doesn't mean everyone has to be!* she seethed. Charly had never married and did not date often.

"Okay," Charly surrendered. She did not approve of what Jeanette had done, but they had to work together. *I need to put my opinions aside.* She felt very sorry for Renee. *Her husband must not have loved her at all. No wonder she turned to suicide.* She led Jeanette back to introduce her to their new assistant – a young girl named Amy.

* * * *

Word traveled fast around the Judicial Center. Confronted in the Hall of Justice dining area again by Jack, he slandered Jeanette, "You heartless bitch!"

On her way to a table, she stopped, holding a Styrofoam plate, with a burger and fries on it, and a soft drink in her hands. "Why are you in my face?" she asked Jack. As before, she looked about in embarrassment and saw many eyes looking at them.

"I just heard about your marriage," he exclaimed, reaching to yank her left hand up, almost spilling her soft drink. "Was this Renee's ring too? You stole her husband. Maybe you don't mind wearing her ring either. What did he do, take it off her body before they lowered it in the ground, and then give it to you?"

Jeanette jerked her hand free from Jack's grasp. "You need to get out of my face and leave me alone, Jack. You're just a sore loser. That's your problem."

"No. You're the loser, Jeanette," he bellowed. "You'll both be sorry! You'll both get what's coming to you. You mark my words!"

He stormed off then. Jeanette knew all eyes were on her. She tried to ignore them as she took a seat in the far corner. She opened up her paperback novel and stuck it in front of her face. *To hell with all of them! No one has ever wanted me to have happiness. Not even my own parents. I don't care what any of them want or think. I've done what I needed to do to have a happy, normal life. They'll just have to accept this or else!*

* * * *

Jack saw Mitchell Peterson as soon as he entered the Judicial Center. Mitchell emptied his pockets of keys and change, and he rushed through the metal detectors with a smug, impatient expression on his face.

Jack wanted to knock that smirk off of his face. In fact, he glared at Mitchell as he gathered his belongings to be on his way. *What's he doing here? He must have come to see Jeanette. More than likely they are going to have lunch together. Maybe squeeze in a quickie in some nearby, cheap motel*, he postulated.

His face set in stone, Mitchell surprised Jack when he approached him. "Have you got a second to talk, deputy?" he asked.

Jack hated this man. The last thing he wanted to do was talk to him. "What do *we* have to talk about?" Jack asked. His blue eyes darkened and his mouth turned downward.

"My wife," Mitchell answered.

"What about her?" Jack challenged, breathing fire. Jack hated Jeanette. He could hardly stand to look at her, but he saw her each day.

"You accosted her yesterday in the cafeteria. I won't have you harassing my wife," Mitchell warned. He moved a step closer to Jack, in his face now.

Jack could smell Mitchell's strong cologne. It almost turned his stomach. *Damn Casanova!* "I'd advise you to get out of my face, Mr. Peterson," Jack ordered. "Or else!" he growled under his breath.

"Or else what?" Mitchell dared. "What are you going to do, take a swing at me? You've already tried to bully a woman. Does it make you feel like a big man to pick on women?"

"Jeanette deserved every word I said to her. She's a cold bitch! And you are a heartless bastard!" Jack professed. He raised his voice a little. The other two deputies took notice.

"Jack, is everything okay?" One of them asked, noting the close proximity of the two men. It looked as if they were about to spar.

"You're on my turf here, Mitchell. I could have you arrested," Jack threatened.

"Go ahead," Mitchell goaded. "I'll have you for false arrest and I'll talk to your supervisor about you threatening my wife. Then we'll see who goes down."

Another of the deputies approached, so Mitchell backed off a bit. "You better watch yourself," he warned Jack in a voice barely above a whisper.

"I'd say that's the other way around, Mr. Peterson. You're the one who better watch his back," Jack threatened.

Mitchell glanced at the other deputy. Then he turned and scurried away, fuming. *If Jack Jordan continues to harass my wife, I'll have his badge*, he secretly vowed.

"What was that all about, Jack," the other deputy asked.

"Nothing to worry about," Jack assured him. "Let's get back to door duty."

As the three deputies took up post at the front doors once more, Jack continued to seethe. *Mitchell and Jeanette make a very fitting couple. I hope the two burn in hell together.* He hoped that day came sooner rather than later.

Chapter 9

Disenchantment

Jeanette and Mitch had been married about six months. Jeanette had made Mitch and Susanna's house her home right after the honeymoon. Now, she rocked Susanna into a peaceful slumber in the nursery.

Ten months old and cutting some more teeth, Susanna fussed a bit more than usual tonight. Jeanette placed her in her crib for the night. She looked up and found Mitch standing in the doorway of the nursery in his bathrobe. His hair was wet, and her nose picked up the fragrances of soap, aftershave, and a touch of cologne. He obviously just got out of the shower. Mitch gave her a come hither smile.

Shit! He wants sex again, Renee comprehended with revulsion. He pestered her every night to have sex with him. Sometimes Jeanette would pleasure Mitch orally, trying to squelch his demands. But then he would suggest they go for Round Two, so he could pleasure her as well. The problem was that there was no pleasure for her. The only pleasure Jeanette received was a good night's sleep and not being hounded by Mitch for sex. Trying to find excuses to put him off on a consistent basis grew old for Jeanette.

Jeanette liked telling people she was married. She liked pointing out that handsome, appealing Mitch was her husband.

She loved telling people that perfect little Susanna was her daughter. She did not even bother with calling herself a 'step'mom anymore. Renee was dead, so she was the only mom Susanna would ever know. Strangers need not know differently. She planned to legally adopt Susanna anyway. Mitch gave his blessing.

Jeanette's fantasy of having a happy little family had materialized, so she resolved to preserve her marriage. So, if she could not come up with a valid excuse to put Mitch off tonight, she would have sex with him. It aggravated her he was so needy in this manner, but for now, she would succumb to his desires.

She walked over and joined him in the doorway. Mitch gathered her in his arms and bestowed a kiss raging with desire. "Why don't you go take a shower and meet me in the bedroom?" he suggested.

You'd think it had been months since we had sex. It was just last night. "Mitch, work today was really hectic. A prosecutor got fired for confronting a juror. Then Susanna is teething, so she was fussy. I'm exhausted," she claimed, rubbing the sides of her temples. "Can I take a rain check on the romance thing until tomorrow night? I'll make it worth your wait," she promised, giving him another lingering kiss and reaching to massage and squeeze his butt cheeks.

"I think I could help you de-stress," he persisted.

"I'm sure you could, darling. But then I'd fall asleep on you. Keep the thoughts for tomorrow," she suggested. "I'm going to go get dressed for bed."

Jeanette slipped out of his arms. She walked down the hallway and went into their bedroom. She quietly shut the door and turned the lock. She would unlock it when she finished changing. She did not want Mitch watching her disrobe. It would only incite his sexual desires all the more.

Mitch watched the door to the bedroom close. He considered joining Jeanette in the bedroom and trying his powers of persuasion once more. But he suddenly found himself more exasperated than aroused.

He abhorred the change he saw in Jeanette. All hot and willing before they married, now, she most always tried to make up an excuse to put him off.

One of his biggest problems in his marriage to Renee had been their lack of intimacy. Mitch decided Jeanette would not shut the door on him sexually. Jeanette was good with Susanna, but things needed to be good between them as well. He would not be turned away by another wife. Jeanette would please him, as he wanted to be pleased, or pay a price.

* * * *

At three in the afternoon, on a Thursday, Jeanette stepped into the Jury Pool Assembly Room to call several potential jurors for a few of the trials going on that day. She told the other jurors, who were not called, they were dismissed for the day.

After she called the last juror number, Jeanette stayed at the podium for a few more moments and watched the remaining un-chosen candidates happily vacate their chairs and head for the exit door. She watched one young man in particular. He had captured her attention all week. Entertaining to watch, he was a real player with the women.

A master list of the juror numbers and names at her fingertips, Jeanette looked up this individual's name: Chad Kennison. Twenty-three years old, he worked at Kennison Enterprises in the East End of Louisville. *Daddy's company,* Jeanette guessed. *He's probably a spoiled rotten, rich kid.*

Chad's appearance each day led credibility to this judgment. He wore a lot of Tommy Hilfiger and Ralph Lauren clothes. Tall, with gleaming blond hair and dazzling blue eyes, everything about this man screamed playboy.

As he passed Jeanette's podium, talking to juror number 185 – Debbie Gray, Jeanette tuned her ear to their conversation. "So...can I talk you into joining me for an early dinner?" she heard Chad ask.

"Thanks. But I'm meeting my boyfriend," his conquest told him. She noted Debbie picked up her pace a little, as if she was trying to shake Chad from her side.

Jeanette left her place at the podium and fell in pace behind them. "I should have figured a pretty girl like you would be taken," Chad commented. His lips spread, displaying a full mouth of gleaming white teeth. "If your boyfriend doesn't treat you right, keep me in mind, okay?"

"Sure," Debbie said with an amused giggle. "Take care," she said, heading toward the sanctuary of the women's restroom, just outside the assembly room to the right.

"You take care too," Chad said. He looked on after her for a second more. Then he headed for the stairway. But before he could bound down the black speckled, granite stairs, another young woman came up the steps toward him. "Stacy! What are you doing here?" he asked. He paused for only a second before he engulfed her in an embrace and gave her a warm kiss.

Aw...this one he knows, Jeanette deduced. *This could get interesting.* She stepped off to the side a bit and continued to scrutinize the couple.

"Who was that woman you were talking to, Chad?" Stacy asked. Her eyes looked perturbed.

I wonder if this is Don Juan's girlfriend, Jeanette mused. She pretended to be looking at a piece of paper she had in her hand, but she kept her ears tweaked to their conversation.

"What woman?" he pretended ignorance.

"The one you just watched go into the women's restroom," Stacy said, pushing herself from Chad's embrace.

"Just a gal who is on jury duty with me. You talk to a lot of folks in there just to pass the time. You aren't jealous are you? You know you are the only one for me, Stacy. We're engaged for gosh sakes." He reached to raise her left hand.

Jeanette saw the huge diamond sparkle. *What a jerk!* she thought, tempted to go over to Chad and his fiancé and tell the girl what she observed Chad doing each day. He was almost constantly on the make.

Debbie came out of the restroom. As she looked Chad's way, Stacy glared at her. Debbie figured Chad was already trying to pick up another woman. She did not care. Already seriously involved with another man and not even remotely interested in Chad Kennison, Debbie looked away and headed toward the stairs.

"I don't know who that bitch thinks she is, but if she is trying to come on to you..." Stacy began to threaten, turning and watching Debbie as she escaped down the stairwell.

"She isn't, Stacy," Chad tried to assure her.

Stupid, naïve girl! It's the other way around! Jeanette's mind screamed. *Someone needs to put this guy in his place.* She held herself back from walking over to them now. *I need to get back to work*, Jeanette decided. She began to walk toward her office. She could not resist glancing back at the couple though. Stacy charged off and Chad raced after her. *You better run, girl. And keep running*, Jeanette pondered. She opened the glass door and entered her office space to get on with the rest of her workday.

* * * *

8:45 a.m. Friday, Deputy Jack stood at the counter talking to Charly, killing some time before they got their day underway. Charly made the comment to Jack that she was glad it was the last day of the week.

"For some of us," he grumbled.

"Are you working tomorrow?" she questioned.

"Yes. Unfortunately. I've been asked to work security for the Savage Pride concert. Mason Greathouse is traveling with his wife and baby girl, so I have to keep an eye out on his tour bus. Just how I want to spend my Saturday," he complained.

"I like their music," Charly admitted. "You can't get me a backstage pass, can you?'

Jeanette perked up her ears, listening from her desk. She would love to have a backstage pass as well.

"You'd have to talk to the show promoter for that. My job is to keep people out, not let them in," Jack clarified.

What a shame, Jeanette thought to herself. She went back to trying to concentrate on work.

"Well, hopefully, you'll enjoy the concert," Charly said with optimism.

"Not hardly. All these rock bands are alike. A bunch of drugged out dregs of society. I wouldn't be surprised if his wife isn't an addicted whore. And the poor kids that get caught in the middle. Remember Eric Clapton's baby that fell off that balcony and died some years ago? I bet mom and dad were so high they forgot the kid existed. Mason Greathouse's daughter will probably be exposed to this same world. So what am I working security for? These people are more danger to themselves than the outside world could ever be to them. Not only should they not be allowed to breed, but they should be exterminated like the roaches they are."

Surprised by mild Jack's angry outburst, Charly pushed her glasses farther back on her nose, as if to take a closer look at him. *He almost sounds as if he hates these people.* His ire and ill will upset her a bit. "Well, I better get to my desk," she said. "I have a few things I need to get together before we go and greet the jury pool this morning," Charly excused herself.

"See ya later," Jack said. He turned, opened the door, and stepped into the hallway. *Charly doesn't like hearing the truth. No one does. This earth is full of such degenerates anymore. It gets worse and worse each day. Each one deserves whatever bad thing happens to them.*

Jack walked off in a bad humor, trying desperately to calm his troubled mind.

Chapter 10

The Voice

Early Saturday morning, just after dawn, Eddie Pierson, a skinny, African American, homeless man, with tattered clothes, and a couple days' beard growth, tottered along an alley in downtown Louisville. The alley ran horizontal with Market and Main Street, situated between Floyd and Brook Streets. Eddie just slept off a bottle of wine.

Eddie headed toward a big dumpster on Market Street. He could scavenger something to eat out of the trash, and he could sell whatever tin cans he could find. Then he could buy himself another bottle of cheap wine. The wine helped to block out the awful voices that often plagued his mind.

As he drew closer, he peeked up a side alley, to the side of the Petrus Restaurant and Nightclub, leading up to Main Street. He saw a man, with his head hanging down, kneeling on the ground beside a sport's car. *Another homeless person?*

He started to ignore him and continue on his important crusade for food and cans. But then he saw something odd on the asphalt. *Is that...it looks a little like blood from here.*

Now Eddie wondered if this man hurt himself. The voices in his head told him, "Ignore that guy. Get yourself some food and cans." And Eddie started to do as they told him.

But his conscience got the best of him. *If I's was hurt, I'd want someone to stop and help me.*

He made his way up this other alley, staying close to the building. He stopped with a jolt as he got close enough to take a good look at this stranger. The black asphalt was colored maroon all around the front of the man. His blood had even run under the car.

"Lord have mercy!" Eddie exclaimed, stumbling back several steps.

He looked all about him as if he expected a killer to jump out. About to make a dash for it, the voice inside his head addressed him, "What's the matter with you, dummy? This isn't some homeless dude like you first thought. He probably has a wallet on him with some cash in it. Cash you could use. You need to check his back pockets and take his cash if he has any. You need it. He sure won't be needing it anymore."

"I...I don't want to go near that's dead body!" Eddie spoke aloud to his unseen demon.

"Don't be a dumbass," it answered back. "Go on, Eddie. Check the guy for his wallet. Then you can run away with cash. You need cash. You were just about to wallow in trash to find some food to eat and cans to sell. Check this guy while you have a chance."

Eddie pressed his fingers into the top of his skull just above his forehead. "Go away!" he ordered the voices.

But they would not leave him. When they came, they pestered him relentlessly until he did what they wanted. "Get the money!" the voices demanded with greater persistence.

"Ow..." Eddie screamed, jerking his hands down from his head. "Alright. Just shut up!" he commanded, lurching forward.

His heart beating out of his chest, he stooped; he struggled to reach behind the dead man and into one of the man's back pockets. Eddie was surprised to see this individual handcuffed to a metal pole that stood near the building.

Thankful to have finally worked the wallet free, Eddie unfolded it. He saw a glimpse of the man's license. But he did not even take time to focus on this item. He did not care who the man was. Eddie only wanted to take his cash and get away from here as quickly as possible.

He pulled open the side pocket. Eddie's eyes lit up as he glimpsed several bills. He pulled forth two twenties, two tens, a five, and two ones – a small fortune to him.

"Jackpot!" the voice happily proclaimed. "Now aren't you glad you listened to me?"

Eddie stashed the cash in one of his threadbare front pockets. He tossed the wallet. It landed with a plop in the blood in front of the man. Horrified once more, Eddie turned and ran away.

* * * *

Jeanette awoke to Mitch kissing her. When he saw her eyes open, he purred in a husky voice, "Good morning, wild woman. Last night was extraordinary! Want to go for Round Two this morning?"

No. I don't, her brain instantly registered. Her repulsion for sex with this man reared its ugly head again, and it reared up with a vengeance. Last night, or actually very early that morning – 1:30 a.m., things vastly differed. *I was excited about other things, so I initiated sex.*

For once, Jeanette seemed to be on a sexual high. Very aggressive, she practically ripped Mitch's clothes off. The deep scratch marks down Mitch's back were a visual reminder.

"Mitch," she whined, pushing him off of her. "What time is it?"

"It's 9:00. What does that matter? It's Saturday."

"I still need to go and check on Susanna," she offered an excuse.

"Susanna is fine. She'll cry if she needs something," Mitch disputed. He went to reach for Jeanette again. But with lightening speed, she sprang from the bed.

Looking down at him, she chastised with a formidable frown, "Put your own selfish desires aside, Mitch. We had our time early this morning. I'm not going to wait until Susanna starts crying. We'd be right in the middle of something, and you'd want me to ignore her. You need to put your daughter first."

Jeanette turned and rushed from the room, not even waiting for Mitch's reply. Mitch rolled over on his back with annoyance. In frustration, he kicked the floral comforter from his body and shielded his eyes from the cheery sunlight coming in the window across the room.

Their physical exchange earlier that morning had been fantastic. But now, Jeanette seemed to have gone cold on him again. Disturbed by this rapid change in her behavior, he could not help but question, *Where'd her appetite come from last night?*

Jeanette had been out with the girls. Girls Night Out, they called it. She came in about 1:15 a.m. She took a shower, and then she entered the bedroom. She had been all over him – hotter than hot!

Now, Mitch felt a little threatened. *Is she not sexually attracted to me anymore? Does it take dancing and flirting with other men to turn her on?* If that was the case, he had an idea to make things better. They could join a swingers' group. This idea appealed to him. In fact, it appealed to him a great deal. *I'll have to talk to Jeanette about it.* Suddenly his morning got better again.

Chapter 11

Juror Number 205

When detectives Roger Matthews and Scott Arnold arrived at the site of the homicide, LMPD and the evidence technicians had already cordoned off the area with bright yellow – **POLICE LINE DO NOT CROSS** – tape. The body had already been moved and placed in a body bag, and its original location and position perfectly sketched in chalk.

The body bag not yet zipped, Scott perused the body. Still not used to looking at real dead bodies, his stomach rolled. He had seen plenty of pictures of them in books, but a deceased human body in the torn flesh was a great deal different than a photograph.

Renee had already been bagged and taken away by the coroner when he had arrived at her murder site. So Scott only saw her dead body in photographs as well. But this new victim was right before him. Scott might have walked past him on the street the day before.

Scott noted the large gash across this man's throat. Potassium content from the breakdown of red blood cells caused a thin film to form over the open eyes and thus make them appear cloudy. These observations chilled Scott.

Lastly, Scott almost shivered, even though it was a warm June day, as he looked below the man's waist and glimpsed the mangled remainder of what had been his genitals. He could not help but feel sympathetic pain in his own lower region.

"See anything interesting, rookie?" Roger's voice jarred him back to the present.

"No. Just sad," Scott commented, pulling his eyes away.

"Yeah, well, don't start crying on me. I didn't bring any tissues," Roger teased in bad taste. "Let's go see what the story is from Matt."

Roger quickly approached Matt Smith, the medical examiner. Scott followed at his heel. A small framed, geeky looking man, Matt wore tiny, black, rectangular framed glasses, with thick lenses. Prone to wearing white, cotton, button down shirts, with small colored squares running throughout, and buttoning every button of the shirt, including the one at his neck, Matt had the appearance of a nerd. Regardless, he was very accomplished at what he did.

"So what have you got for us, Matt?" Roger asked him. Scott was standing just to the side of him.

"The vic's name is Chad Kennison. He's twenty-three, and it appears from his state of rigor mortis, hypostasis and body temp he's been dead about ten hours. Cause of death: A knife wound to the carotid, causing him to bleed out. The perp also handcuffed him to a post and mutilated his genitals, so it appears we have a sexual element to the crime as well. His jeans were unbuttoned and unzipped and his underwear lowered. The team is collecting evidence for DNA testing. I'll, of course, be performing an autopsy. We'll turn over all our findings to you."

"Thanks," Roger said. "Who called this in?"

"One of the kids from the fast food restaurant over there," he pointed toward the building. "They came out to put some garbage in the dumpster and found him. The kid's pretty shook up. He went back inside."

"Okay. We'll go question him next."

Roger started away toward the restaurant and Scott followed. He did not suspect they would gain much knowledge from the kid who found the victim, but they always followed up every possible lead.

* * * *

After Roger and Scott left the crime scene, they went to question Chad's parents. His parents had already been notified of their son's death. Located in east Louisville in the Lake Forest subdivision, Chad's parents called a sizeable, two-story, brick house their home. Chad had resided there as well.

Ralph parked his Impala on the street in front of the residence. He and Scott walked up the long driveway, passing several expensive cars – a Volvo, a Mazda sport's car and a Saab. They climbed three steps and approached a fancy double door. Each door showcased a shiny brass handle and large, frosted, oval glass lined in pearl.

Roger rang the doorbell. He could hear it's impressive, loud, baritone chime. They both waited patiently for several minutes. A tall, blond-haired man with prominent blue eyes answered the door.

Chad's father, Scott assessed. The image of Chad's dead body came to mind again. Even though his eyes had been cloudy, they were a mirror image of this older man.

"Mr. Kennison?" Roger questioned.

"Yes," he replied. He looked from Roger to Scott, scrutinizing them both. He noted Roger's slightly wrinkled suit, his crooked tie, and his rustled gray hair with a bit of disdain. Scott, on the other hand, got his stamp of approval. His suit crisp and tailored to fit him; his tie impeccably knotted and straight; his black shoes polished; his hair neatly set in place; Scott's image fit into their elite social circle. Mr. Kennison wore a pale blue, Izod, golf shirt and seamless, tan slacks.

"I'm Detective Matthews. This is Detective Arnold. We're with the Homicide Squad. We've been assigned to your son's case," Roger briefly explained.

"So what do you know? Who did this to my boy?" Mr. Kennison asked, his voice cracking. He no longer cared about these men's appearances. He only wanted them to give him answers.

"We haven't determined that yet, sir" Roger confessed. "But, if you wouldn't mind, we'd like to ask you and your wife some questions to aid in our investigation."

"Mind? No, of course, we wouldn't mind. We want the monster who did this caught and punished," Mr. Kennison declared. He stepped back a few paces. "Come in. My wife is in the great room with some of our family."

Roger and Scott followed him down a hallway and into the great room. Two women sat on a cream-colored, floral, Queen Anne sofa. One had her arm around the other and appeared to be quietly wishing condolences. Scott guessed the woman being softly spoken to must be Mrs. Kennison.

Across the room by the massive stone fireplace, another couple stood. A large, exquisitely framed, Kennison family photograph hung above the fireplace. It appeared Chad had been there only child.

A young girl sat in a Queen Anne chair across from the sofa. Tears ran down her face. Scott could not help but notice her short red hair. *We need to find out who this woman is.* The evidence technicians gathered some red hairs at the crime scene. These hairs had been sent off for DNA testing.

"Norma," Mr. Kennison addressed. One of the women on the sofa looked up at him. "These are the detectives who are investigating Chad's murder. They want to ask us some questions."

"What can *we* tell them?" she asked. She looked ill – her brown hair was frazzled; her green eyes glazed; her complexion pale; her lips two white lines pressed together.

"We can tell them whatever they need to help catch our son's killer," he answered with determination.

"What kind of a person could do such a terrible thing?" Mrs. Kennison lamented, looking from her husband, to Roger, to Scott. The lady beside her squeezed her hand, looking at the detectives now too. She had a very pained expression on her face. Both women were clothed in dresses, even though it was Saturday.

"That's exactly what we are trying to determine," Roger answered. "Do you mind if we talk to the two of you alone? This shouldn't take long."

"That's fine," Mr. Kennison agreed. "Sam, Martina, Angela...you don't mind going in another room, do you?"

"No," they all answered, almost in unison.

Scott thought it a little strange Mr. Kennison had not addressed the young woman sitting in the chair. *Who is she?* She looked to be around the same age as Chad.

"Should I leave to?" This woman asked, looking bewildered. She had on a bright white, smooth skirt and a baby blue, short sleeved blouse. Sandals on her feet gave her a more casual look than the other women.

"No, Stacy," Mr. Kennison was quick to tell her. "You were Scott's fiancé. You are family too."

Hearing this woman was Scott's fiancé, Roger and Scott exchanged a quick, suspecting glance. Thinking of the short, curly red hairs discovered at the crime scene, questions raced through Scott's mind. Excited, he thought they might be on the brink of solving this case. *It can't be this easy.*

"Th…thanks, Bob," the young girl said. A few more tears ran down her face as she stood, walked over to the couch, and sat down beside Chad's mom. Chad's dad went and sat on the other side of her.

Roger took a seat in the Queen Anne chair Stacy just vacated and Scott sat in another to its side. The chairs were separated by a round cherry table with a large, antique, oil lamp on it. Scott looked at the wall across from him and took note of three, giant, glass display cases – one filled with crystal pieces, another with china, and another with porcelain dolls and other knickknacks. Pursuant to the location and size of the house, the expensive furniture, and collectibles, Chad's parents appeared wealthy.

"Okay. If you don't mind, I'd like to start by asking Stacy a few questions," Roger told them. "Young lady, your first name is Stacy, correct? Can I also get your last name, just for the record?"

"Yes. I'm Stacy Prescott," she answered. She made sweeping eye contact with Roger before looking down to fiddle with her engagement ring.

It was then Scott noticed a missing fingernail on her right hand. His heart sped up a bit more. *She's missing a fingernail, and the techs found one at the crime scene! Too big of a coincidence for us to ignore.* He slid to the end of his chair and impatiently listened as Roger continued his interrogation, anxious to share his important discovery with his partner.

"And you were Chad's fiancé, correct? How long were the two of you engaged?"

Stacy looked back up at Roger and answered, "We got officially engaged…with the ring…" She glanced back down at it and fingered it again. Then looking back up, she continued, "about six months ago. But we've been a pledged couple since my coming out party when I was sixteen. I'm twenty-two, so we've been a couple for six years."

"Did...did you say...your coming *out* party?" Scott repeated in surprise, sliding back in his chair again.

"She means when she *came out* to society at the Debutante Ball," Scott's mother explained, seeing the perplexed expression on Scott's face. "It's when young ladies in our social circle are paired with eligible young men in our community. Chad and Stacy were matched and pledged to marry some day. Chad made it binding when he presented Stacy with an engagement ring and officially asked her to be his wife six months ago. They were supposed to marry in October – four months from now." Her voice trailed off and sounded hollow as she concluded her explanation.

A few tears ran down Stacy's face. Chad's dad put his arm around her shoulder and patted her arm. Scott meticulously studied her. *Is she crying because she's sad Chad's dead, or because of her guilt?*

"Stacy, were you out with Chad the night of his murder?" Roger continued his interrogation, hardly seeming to have missed a beat. He sat up ramrod straight in his chair with his hands folded over his abdomen.

Stacy wiped the tears away, cleared her throat, and looked Roger in the eye again. She seemed to be struggling to regain her composure. "N...no. He is...w...was...on jury duty. I talked to him when he left the courthouse...about 6:45. He was almost picked to serve on a jury. He had been in a courtroom being questioned by both the defense and prosecution. But when it was all said and done, he wasn't chosen. He said he was going to grab some dinner. That was the last I heard from him," she relayed. "I still can't believe he's gone," she added in a tiny, barely audible voice. She stared into her lap once more.

"So were you at home when Chad called you?" Roger asked, staring intently at her.

"Yes," Stacy answered. She avoided making eye contact when she made this statement. Roger knew they could verify whether Stacy was home or not by pulling phone records if need be.

"What does it matter where Stacy was?" Chad's father asked with a disapproving grimace. "What's this got to do with finding Chad's killer?"

"We have to account for everyone's whereabouts that night, Mr. Kennison," Roger explained, shifting his eye contact briefly to Mr. Kennison.

"Stacy, do you live alone?" He fired another question, eyeballing her once again.

"No. I still live with my parents," she answered. She looked a little uncomfortable now. Chad's dad looked aggravated.

"Were your parents at home with you?"

"Yes, sir," she answered.

"Would you mind if we took a fingerprint and DNA sample from you?"

"Okay...that's enough!" Chad's father proclaimed. He sprang to his feet and approached Roger. Swinging his finger in his face, he declared, "I've seen enough movies to know you cops always try to pin the murder on someone in the family first. That is ridiculous in this case. If you are even trying to suggest Stacy had anything...anything whatsoever...to do with Chad's death, then you are crazy as hell! You can both leave if you came here to badger any of us...me, my wife, or Stacy. Have you got that?!"

"I do," Roger told him, keeping his voice calm and his eyes carefully planted on Mr. Kennison.

Scott nervously watched Mr. Kennison. He did not know if he was going to take a swing at Roger. He seemed dangerously near to doing so.

"This is all preliminary – standard procedure – so calm down," Roger tried to explain.

"Don't try to play me for a fool. Asking a few innocent questions is preliminary. Asking for fingerprints and a DNA sample is not. What do you want this for?" he demanded to know.

"To rule Stacy out as a suspect," Roger admitted. "Mr. Kennison, we found short, red hairs by Chad's body. We merely need to confirm these did *not* belong to Stacy. A simple DNA test would rule her out."

"I...I would n...never hurt Chad," Stacy proclaimed. Her face turned red as a beet, and she trembled.

"Don't say another word, Stacy," Chad's father cautioned her. "You do *not* have to take a DNA sample from Stacy. She is *not* a suspect. That is ludicrous! You need to leave my house, and don't come back unless you have news about the *real* killer," he demanded.

"Mr. Kennison, we are only trying to find out who is responsible for your son's murder..."

"No you're not. You are trying to *pin* my son's murder on an innocent young woman. My son deserves justice, not laziness. You both disgust me. Now, get out of my house, or I'll call my attorney and get him started on a harassment case against you."

Roger stood then. Scott followed suit. "Thank you, Mr. Kennison," he said, still being cordial. He headed toward the front door, Scott right behind him. Mr. Kennison followed them both. Scott's could almost feel the man's hot breath on his neck he was so close.

As soon as Scott cleared the doorway, Mr. Kennison slammed the door and locked it. "Whew...I thought he was going to slug you," Scott said to Roger as he dropped in beside him. Roger hurried up the driveway, heading to the car.

"Well, regardless of bulldog Kennison's interference, we *will* get a DNA sample from Stacy. We'll have to do it the hard way. We'll get a search warrant, take fingerprints, a DNA sample, and search Stacy Prescott's house for anything else incriminating," Roger said, both to Scott and to himself.

"Did you happen to notice Stacy was missing a fingernail?" Scott asked with relish. "I believe she may be our murderer. Or if not, at the very least, she is lying about not being with Chad that night."

"I know. I noticed the missing fingernail as well." Roger rained on Scott's parade. "That's a bit damning, but fingerprints, and especially DNA, will tell the story," Roger replied. "Let's get the paperwork rolling."

"Sounds like a plan," Scott agreed as they both climbed into the car. They were on their way within minutes.

* * * *

Saturday evening, Roger and Scott went to Petrus – the nightclub on Main Street by Bridges Smith and Company – to question individuals there about what they might know. The bouncer confessed having seen Chad with a woman who had short, curly, red hair.

Could this woman have been Stacy Prescott? Roger was still not certain. He and Scott would not know for certain until they obtained a DNA sample from Stacy and saw if it matched to the DNA found at the crime scene.

The crime lab in Frankfort was very backed up, and Roger and Scott realized it might be several months before they had any results back. They decided to take their time in obtaining DNA samples from Stacy, so as not to spook her or her family.

Chapter 12

Killer's Mind

Early Monday – 1:00 a.m., he still savored Chad Kennison's murder. Once again, it all came much too easy. He heard through the grapevine a homeless, schizophrenic black man might be brought in for questioning. He found this scenario hilarious. *Wouldn't it be grand if the murder got pinned on some crazy, good-for-nothing, homeless person? This would be too sweet!* he considered with gaiety.

As with Renee's murder, he kept replaying Chad's slaying in his mind. He believed, in both instances, justice had been served. Neither of these two people – Renee, an ungrateful bitch, or Chad, a sex-starved, spoiled rich boy – deserved to take up space and breathe. He did the world a favor. Chad's death a blessing in disguise, his perverted urges got him killed. *They should pin a metal on me. I'm making society a better place to live,* he chuckled to himself.

He lay in bed, but not sleeping. Keyed up, images vividly played in his mind. He relaxed and enjoyed them. After all, justice was one part of his killings, but the high he got from pulling them off was the other.

Young stud, Chad, didn't waste any time accompanying me into the alley. In fact, Chad was all over me all evening. As we left the club, Chad put his arms around my waist, pulled me

79

*close, and pressed his disgusting, aroused dick against my butt.
My plan was to kill him, but Chad's degrading actions gave me
another brainstorm. I'll cut off his dick.*

Excitement surged through him as he recalled it. He had
hardly been able to wait to inflict this *special*, painful injury.
He had punished Chad as well as killed him.

He and Chad had stopped beside Chad's sports car. He
had not accounted for the light from the parking garage on the
other side of the alley when he had planned out this murder. It
had been daylight, so he assumed the alley would be dark.

As it was, being between Chad's car and the wall
partially hid them from view. He suggested Chad park in this
particular space, near the back of the alley, for this very reason.
Another reason was the metal pole beside the wall.

Chad could not wait for it all to begin. *When I
suggested I handcuff his arms to that pole, Chad didn't object.
He got kinky pleasure out of it. Chad's just a step above an
animal*, he thought with rage and repugnance.

He had unzipped Chad's pants, lowered Chad's
underwear, and dropped to his knees in front of Chad to put his
plan into action. As he orally pleasured Chad and watched him
lose himself in ecstasy, he obscurely reached into the bag he
had sat on the ground beside him. He pulled forth a sharp, six-
inch, utility knife – *His* turn to be excited.

He pleasured Chad some more, bringing him almost to
the point of no return. Chad's eyes closed and his head fell
back. He raised the knife and he slashed. "Oh...f...fuck!"
Chad shouted. Chad's head snapped forward; his eyes popped
open; he lurched frontward. The handcuffs kept him from
going anywhere.

*I sprang upwards then, plunging the knife into the
center of Chad's throat. I felt the knife strike bone before I*

jerked it from side to side. After he opened the streaming gash all across Chad's neck, he wrenched the knife free.

Chad began to slowly slide down the pole. *I heard voices then.* He looked up, in alarm. Another couple walked up the alley toward them. *I had to think fast. I grabbed Chad's body, pressed against it, and held it upright.* He wanted it to appear they engaged in an intimate embrace. Chad's body jerked, and he made strange gurgling noises. *I held tight to him. He became dead weight, as the life seeped out of him. But I could not let him fall. I could not draw attention from these other people.*

The other couple stopped a few cars up. They were laughing and talking and oblivious to anyone else being in the alley. They got into a pickup truck. He watched them start the truck and pull out. The truck passed by them and turned into the alley behind the building. When it disappeared from sight, he released Chad's body. *My heart hammered in my chest. I panted. But the chance of almost getting caught, but still getting away with Chad's murder, made it that much more exciting and fulfilling.*

He watched Chad's body slide down the pole. His knees eventually hit with a thud onto the hard, bloody blacktop. All was silent. Chad Kennison ceased to exist.

He grabbed his bag and forced himself to scurry away. He went behind the building. He tossed the knife up on the loading dock. It landed with a clang.

He reached underneath to retrieve a black garbage bag he had stashed there earlier. He pulled forth a thick, clean towel. He laid the towel on another dock.

He pulled off his blood-saturated sweater, kicked off his shoes, slipped out of his bloody slacks, and pulled off his thin, white – now stained red – dinner gloves. He tossed all the items except the shoes on top of the knife. Keeping his ears vigilantly tuned for the sound of any other intrusions, he heard nothing. He could vaguely hear the muted sound of music coming from the Petrus Nightclub. *It's after midnight. No one hangs around back here in the alley at this hour. No one but a killer.*

He picked up the towel and carefully cleaned off his arms, legs, chest and neck. He scrubbed his face, and lastly, he wiped off his navy shoes. *At least, with them being such dark shoes, if I miss anything, the blood won't show.*

He reached back into the trash bag. He pulled forth a clean sweater and slacks. He quickly redressed and slipped back on his shoes.

He circumspectly wrapped all of the bloody items in the bulky towel and stashed them in the trash bag. He picked up the trash sack and his other bag, and he began walking toward the parking garage on the corner.

He passed the alley where Chad was again. He took one more second to gloat. *Mission accomplished*, he thought with glee. He hurried off to his car, conveniently parked in the parking garage on the corner.

Chapter 13

The Interrogation

The fingerprint analysis, conducted on the print lifted from Chad Kennison's wallet, had garnered a match. Roger called the Commonwealth Attorney's office.

"Darrell Adams," he answered, after his receptionist put through the call.

"Hey, Darrell, how's it going? It's Roger," he began with pleasantries.

"Everything's okay in my world. What's up in yours?" he asked.

"I need a warrant for the arrest of Eddie Pierson. He's an African American, homeless, schizophrenic. His fingerprints have been identified as those lifted from Chad Kennison's wallet."

"The young guy found near Petrus?" Darrell verified.

"That's the one."

"I'll get you your warrant," he vowed. "You guys just get me the killer."

"Hey, that warrant won't be necessary," Scott called out to Roger from his desk. He just hung up his own phone when he overheard Roger's conversation.

"Hang on a minute, Darrell," Roger said, lowering the receiver and looking toward Scott for clarification.

"Eddie Pierson is voluntarily coming in with some LMPD officers. He flagged them down in an alley near the Wayside Mission. We may have to wait until he sobers up a bit, but then we can question him and see what he knows about Chad's death."

"Great!" Roger chirped. "Darrell, an LMPD officer is bringing in Eddie now. He wants to talk to us. I'll keep you informed as to what we uncover."

"I'll be waiting," Darrell told him.

Roger hung up the phone then. He was anxious for them to bring in Eddie.

* * * *

The interrogation room – a small, dismal area, with deliberately dim, flickering, fluorescent lighting – contained a four foot table and three, fabric-padded chairs. On the wall, above the table, hung a white, dry erase board. The other three sides of the room donned plain, neutral walls. A single, locked door led into the hallway. A hidden camera monitored the room.

Eddie Pierson sat facing the blank wall in the back. He whimpered and whined and held his head. To make Eddie feel more comfortable, Roger took his suit jacket off and placed it on the back of the chair. He also loosened his tie. He sat down in a chair beside Eddie, facing the dry erase board. Scott stood by the back wall.

Scott wanted to take his suit jacket off as well. He wanted to wrap it around his face to try and muffle the strong, offensive smell in the room. Instead, he attempted to hold his breath. Eddie smelled horrible. The combination of rancid body odor, filth, and stale alcohol turned Scott's stomach. He was amazed Roger could sit so close to Eddie.

"Hello, Eddie. It's been awhile," Roger greeted.

Eddie's criminal activity record being rather extensive, he had been in and out of trouble since his teen years. His list of crimes included petty theft, breaking and entering, and a single episode of assault. Other than the one assault charge, most of his illegal actions were not violent in nature.

Diagnosed with schizophrenia in his early twenties, Eddie spent time, on and off, in mental institutions and halfway houses his entire adult life. He would turn thirty this year, although he looked much older.

"I knew I...I's shouldn't have...have...touched that dead body," he rattled. "Bad! The voices tell me to do bad things. It's wasn't my fault."

"What exactly did the voices tell you to do, Eddie?" Roger asked in a steady, level voice. Eddie was tremendously agitated. He did not want to spook him and send him into an unresponsive psychotic episode.

"They...he was just kneeling there with blood all around him. I was gonna run off; ya know? But the voices...they's told me to rob him. I didn't wanna touch him; ya know? I'm sorry. Don't's throw me in that jail cell with all's those mean people. Please!" he pleaded. He rolled his head from side to side in his hands.

"Now, Eddie, nobody said anything about throwing you in a jail cell. We just want to ask you some questions, that's all," Roger tried to calm him.

"Ya mean it?" he questioned.

The voices chipped in, "Don't trust him."

"Shut the fuck up!" Eddie demanded, balling his fist and tapping himself in the side of the head. "You's already gotten me in enough trouble."

"Are the voices talking to you now, Eddie?" Roger questioned.

"They's always talkin' to me. The only way to get them to be quiet for awhile is to drink until I's pass out. Could I's have something to drink?"

"I can get you some water if you want," Roger told him. "But no alcohol. The sooner you answer our questions, the sooner we can get you out of here. Okay?"

"Okay," Eddie said, rocking back and forth in his chair. "What's you wanna know?"

"What time did you find the dead man?"

"It was early; you know? The sun was just comin' up. I's slept off a bottle of wine. I's goin' to a dumpster; you know? I's gonna find somethin' to eat and maybe some cans to sell. I seen the guy kneelin' between a car and the wall; you know? I's thought he was another homeless guy, like me; you know? I's went to pass him, and that's when...that's when...I...I's seen all the blood. I's just wanted to get out of there; you know? But the voices wouldn't let me. They said I's be stupid if I's didn't see if the guy had any cash on him. So I's reached in his pocket, finds his wallet, takes his cash, tosses the wallet and runs off. I's spent some of the money on somes good wine and a little food; you know? I's have some left. I's give you what I have," he fished in his pocket and pulled forth a few dirty, crumpled bills. "I's know what I's did was wrong...but...the voices..." Eddie began to wail again. He tossed the money on the table in front of him.

Roger ignored the cash. Instead he continued the interrogation. "So the guy was dead when you found him, right, Eddie?"

"Yeah. That's right," Eddie confirmed.

The voices asked, "Are you sure? Maybe you killed him."

"I's didn't kill him!" Eddie proclaimed to the empty chair beside him.

The voices accused, "Maybe you just thought you were sleeping. Maybe you killed him, and you are blocking it out."

"No! No!" Eddie exclaimed. He sprang to his feet and sent the chair sailing in Scott's direction. Scott jumped aside, and the chair hit the wall with a loud bang. "I's not blockin' anything out. I's passed out drunk the night before. I's did not kill that man!"

"Eddie," Roger called, himself standing.

Scott gaped at Eddie, trying to determine what he should do. He had never dealt with a mentally ill person before. He watched Roger closely. He would follow his lead. If he tried to restrain Eddie, he would assist.

"It ain't true. You's cain't listen to them," Eddie told Roger. "The's only thing I's done was to take the man's wallet. He's already handcuffed to that pole and kneelin' in a pool of blood. I's didn't hurt him. I swear."

"Okay, Eddie. I believe you," Roger tried to assure him. "Why don't you have a seat again? We are going to see if we can arrange to have you taken somewhere."

"Where?" he asked in fear.

"You want the voices to be quiet, don't you?" Roger inquired.

"Yeah," Eddie replied.

"Okay. I can help you with that. But you need to go back on some meds."

The voices reminded him, "Oh, you're screwed now! You'll be drugged again. You'll go through withdrawal because they won't let you drink at those hospitals,"

"No! Don't's send me to the hospital! I's be good. I's promise. I's need a drink!" he wailed. He plopped into the other chair. Eddie grabbed his knees, lowered his head into his lap, and rocked back and forth.

Roger figured he was done talking to Eddie for the day. He motioned to Scott to follow him out of the room. Scott headed toward the door and Roger quickly followed. They shut the door behind them. It automatically locked.

In the hall, Scott sighed and said, "I thought he was going to turn violent toward you for a moment."

"No. Eddie's mentally ill, but he isn't really the violent type. The one charge of assault on his record was more self-defense than anything. I think he's telling the truth," Roger told him.

"But what if his illness caused him to kill this man?" Scott questioned. "Are we just going to cut him loose?"

"No. We are going to have him committed to Central State for the time being. In the meantime, we need to wait for the DNA analysis to come back from the state crime lab. That will take a few months. Once we get this data back, we'll determine whether we need to arrest Eddie for this crime. DNA talks."

"Sounds right," Scott was quick to agree.

He wished he could go take a shower. The odor from the interrogation room seemed to have followed them out. It appeared to be lodged in his sinuses. Scott was relieved to be through with Eddie.

They looked up to see Abe, another homicide detective approaching them. "Roger, Scott, sorry to interrupt; But there was a call from Preston and Market. One of the employees found some bloody clothes and a knife, by the dumpster. I thought these items might pertain to the Chad Kennison homicide."

"Thanks, Abe," Roger said with a smile. "Come on, Scott, let's roll," he directed his partner.

Scott hurried across the room with Roger.

"Sounds like our killer wasn't too smart," Roger proclaimed. "Could it be a young girl got rid of bloody clothes and a knife in a hurry? Ditching them a street over?"

"You still think Stacy?" Scott questioned.

"Oh, yeah. Until her DNA rules her out, she's our prime suspect." They rushed from the building then.

* * * *

Some LMPD officers and evidence technicians were already investigating the bloody discovery when Roger and Scott arrived at Preston & Market minutes later. Roger wasted no time getting into the thick of things. "What have we got here?" he asked Christopher Hughes, who was already photographing the evidence and bagging it up.

Christopher Hughes handled at least some of the gathering of physical evidence at most homicide scenes. His short black hair, that he kept spiked with heavy hair gel, made him look more like a punk rocker than an evidence technician. "We have a towel, bloody clothes, gloves and a knife. My hunch is the blood on these items will match to the Chad Kennison homicide."

"That's our hunch too," Roger revealed. "Was it in the dumpster?"

"That's where a sanitation worker who found it believes it originated. He said homeless folks scavenger in this dumpster on almost a daily basis. He thinks someone tossed this bag out to get to food or cans or whatever. He started to just throw the bag back in, but the blade of the knife tore the bag and was sticking out. When he saw the bloody clothes along with the knife, he jumped back in his truck and called the police on his cell." Christopher pointed to the man. He stood by his truck, smoking a cigarette, and watching all the police action around him.

"Do you have any idea how often the dumpster is emptied?"

"He said on a daily basis, early in the morning. He said he was off on the weekend, ill. So he thinks the bag was likely sitting there all weekend. But no one took the time to throw it back in the dumpster. So if no one else cleaned up, the bag might have been sitting there since the morning after Chad's murder."

"Sounds like a pretty feasible theory to me," Roger agreed. "You send this stuff to the lab and get me some DNA results. Any fingerprints you can lift would be great too."

"As to fingerprints, I might be able to get something from the gloves. But I'll make you no promises," Christopher said. "I'll be in touch though."

"We'll be waiting for your call, Christopher," Roger told him. "Let's go question the sanitation worker," he said to Scott, and started heading toward his truck.

As they walked away, Scott mused over why the killer left behind the bloody shoes they already recovered from the murder scene. *He discarded everything else incriminating in the garbage bag we just recovered. Maybe the shoes somehow fell out*, he conjectured. Lost in thought, he made his way, with Roger, toward the man that found the garbage bag.

* * * *

Surprised when she saw Scott step into the Jury Assembly Hall, Debbie stood as she saw his eyes scanning the room. *Is he looking for me, or is he here for some other purpose?* she wondered. His wide smile, upon seeing her, told her all she needed to know. She excused herself to folks sitting in chairs at the end of her row. She squeezed in front of them, making her way out. She headed toward Scott.

"Scott, what are you doing here?" she asked with a pleased grin as she approached him.

"Um…I was in the neighborhood," he teased. Since his office was only a block over, this statement was true. He took a second to appraise Debbie. Dressed in jeans and a T-shirt, with her hair pulled back in a ponytail, she still looked adorable to Scott. "So aren't you glad today is Monday? Only four more days and you'll get to escape this room, and all the waiting to possibly be picked for a jury, for good. And you'll get to see me later this evening."

"The last part is the best," she flirted.

"Excuse me," Jeanette said, as she came into the room. Scott and his girlfriend partially blocked the doorway. When she got a good look at Scott, she said, "Detective Arnold?"

"Yes. How are you? I'm not here on official business today. I just came by to say a few words to my girlfriend. This is her last week of jury duty. You guys treat her right, okay?"

Jeanette gave the woman at his side a brief perusal. "We'll certainly try and see she is taken care of," she responded with a slight smile. "Now, if you'll excuse us, I need to call some more potential jurors."

"Oh…of course," Scott conceded. "Debbie, I will see you this evening," he said. His eyes bright and joyful and his dimples showing, Scott bent to give Debbie a quick kiss. Then he turned to leave the room.

Someone is going to get lucky tonight, Jeanette crudely concluded. She took her place behind the podium and watched Debbie sashay back across the room, heading for the seat she vacated. *My husband would make a special trip to see me too if he thought he would get lucky that night*, she thought with aversion. *Men are like peas in a pod. They all focus on one thing.*

Jeanette loved Susanna from the bottom of her heart, but she almost hated Mitch. She went through the motions of having sex with him at least once a week to stop his pathetic pleading. She even joined a swinger's group at Mitch's insistence. But she garnered no enjoyment from any of it. Fortunately, Jeanette found other ways to pleasure herself when he was not around. Otherwise, she believed she would lose her mind.

"Alright, folks, it's time to call some more potential jurors," she addressed the jury pool. She needed to put her personal thoughts aside and get on with the business of the day. She took one more look at Debbie, and then proceeded to attend to the rest of her audience.

* * * *

Jeanette approached Debbie in the dining area at the Hall of Justice at lunchtime the next day. "Mind if I sit with you?" she asked.

"No. Of course not," Debbie replied with a friendly smile. "It'd be good to have someone to talk to. Jury duty is hard because of all the waiting…and waiting…and waiting. I wish there was a way you could let us go to work and call us there if we were needed. I'm Debbie Gray, by the way. Your name was…Jeanette?"

"Yes. I'm Jeanette. The last name is O'Riley." Proud of her Irish heritage, one of the few things in her birthright she was happy with, she pointed out, "Thus the ivory complexion, bright blue eyes and red hair." Her lips curved upwards, and a small chortle escaped. "I know what you mean about jury duty. Most people have the same complaints as you do," Jeanette agreed. She sat down across from Debbie. She sat her plate, containing a sandwich and chips, and a drink, on the table. "So what do you do for a living?"

"I work for CASA…"

"Oh, the children's advocate group. That's great," Jeanette commented, taking a bite of her ham sandwich. She quietly chewed. Then she commented, "So you and Detective Arnold are both involved in helping people then."

"Yeah. We are," Debbie concurred with a contented grin.

Jeanette took a second to study this other woman's face. Debbie had a perfect rosy complexion – not a blemish on it. She looked like a model for a makeup or soap commercial. Her prettiest feature – her big, green eyes – glowed. The black hair which framed Debbie's face made her eyes stand out all the more.

"Seeing Detective Arnold again yesterday gave me a bit of a start," Jeanette admitted.

"Why?" Debbie asked, taking a bite of her own sandwich: roast beef.

"The last time I saw him was when he and his partner came here to tell my manager and I that our office assistant, Renee Peterson, had died. Actually, she committed suicide. Stood on a train track and let the train hit her. How crazy is that?"

"Oh…yes, Scott mentioned that," Debbie revealed. "He had a hard time believing she committed suicide."

"He did. Why?" Jeanette questioned. She put her sandwich down and gave Debbie her full attention, interested in what Debbie had to say.

"It's just such a brutal way for a woman to commit suicide, that's all. Scott had a hard time accepting this was the way it was."

"So is he still investigating Renee's death?" Jeanette inquired, taking a drink of her soda.

"No. His boss closed the case a long time ago. All the evidence pointed to suicide, according to Scott. It *is* hard to believe a woman would choose to die that way though," Debbie remarked, sticking a pretzel in her mouth.

"Yeah. We all had a hard time believing it too," Jeanette told her, breaking eye contact for the first time in several moments.

"I bet," Debbie said. "Suicide is such a horrible thing."

"Yes. It is," Jeanette agreed. She paused, silent for a moment. Then she looked back up, forced a smile and said, "Gosh...I didn't mean to get off on such a depressing subject. Detective Arnold seems like a very nice man. It was kind of him to stop by to see you this morning. Seems like it's serious between the two of you."

"It is," Debbie admitted, with a gleeful chuckle. "Just between the two of us, I think Scott may propose before long."

"How wonderful!" Jeanette cooed. "I hope it's sooner rather than later. Because the two of you seem to make the ideal couple."

"Thanks," Debbie replied. "So I take it you are married," she said, looking at the ring and wedding band on Jeanette's left hand.

"Yes. And I have a beautiful daughter," Jeanette proclaimed. She pulled her purse off the corner of her chair. She unzipped one of the compartments and fished for her change purse. She opened it and pulled forth some pictures. This is my husband, Mitchell, and my daughter, Susanna," she said pointing to a family photo of the three of them. She also showed Debbie some pictures of Susanna by herself.

"She is precious!" Debbie clucked. "And your husband is very handsome."

"Thank you. I agree with you on both counts," Jeanette declared. Debbie handed Jeanette back her photos. Jeanette glanced at the family picture, before she stashed the photo holder back in her change purse and returned it to her handbag.

Jeanette loved showing family photos. They looked like the perfect family in it, even if Mitch did make her skin crawl sometimes. Jeanette still made her marriage work, and that was what counted. In fact, her legal adoption of Susanna would be final in a few days.

"Well, it's almost one o'clock. I guess I better be getting back to the jury pool room. It was nice talking to you," Debbie said.

"I enjoyed talking with you too. Take care, Debbie. And good luck on your relationship with Detective Arnold."

"Thanks," Debbie said, as she slid back her chair and got up. She gathered her trash from the table and started away.

Jeanette watched her walk across the room, throw her trash in a trash container, and hurry out the door. *She seems like a nice lady. I bet she is a good lay too. Must be if Detective Arnold is considering marriage. That's what it's all about for men – whoever is the best lay. Good luck, Debbie. You'll need it*, Jeanette thought with considerable irritation. She stuck her sandwich in her mouth and subconsciously tore into it.

Chapter 14

Details

A few months later, on a Saturday, Roger sat at his desk reading the forensics report on the Chad Kennison murder. He had just got it back from the State Crime Lab in Frankfort, Kentucky. Most of Louisville's DNA testing and fingerprinting analysis was done there, although some was done in private labs within the city.

DNA testing, on saliva found on Chad's dismembered penis and short red hairs discovered on his jeans and by the dock area in back of Bridges Smith and Company, showed they belonged to someone other than Eddie. This other individual's DNA tested male, which made for an interesting twist to the case.

Saliva in Chad's genital area indicated another man had been orally satisfying him before he died. They also found semen at the crime scene matching to Chad's DNA. Roger concluded Chad must have been gay. A gay bar, Connections, was only a block away from the homicide scene. It seemed plausible Chad might have left this club with a gay man.

However, it appeared his murderer may have been a woman. They also found other, short, red hairs that tested female. They lifted a small, seemingly female, palm print from Chad's right shoulder, and a manicured, fake fingernail was found lodged in the wound in Chad's neck. Bloody, female, shoe prints led back toward a dock area behind Bridges Smith & Company. The pair of shoes that made the prints were also found discarded behind this building.

So the evidence suggested one woman and one man – one of them sexually – had contact with the victim before he died. What Roger and Scott needed to determine was if Chad's male sexual partner, or a female – possibly Stacy – or even Eddie, killed him. He and Scott would go over to Connections this evening to question the bartenders, bouncers, and some of the patrons. They were in hopes one of them could shed some light on who the man with the short, red hair might have been.

The DNA testing on the items found in the garbage bag at Preston & Market had not come back yet. It was being done at a private lab in Louisville on Chamberlain Lane. They hoped to have the results of these tests back soon as well.

"Hey, Scott," Roger called to his partner. "Here are the results from the DNA testing done on the evidence found at the Chad Kennison crime scene. As you'll see, the report identifies both a man and a woman at the crime scene. You and I are going to try and find out who the man and woman are with the short, red hair. If we determine these individuals have a firm alibi, then we'll look at Eddie again."

"Okay," Scott agreed.

"Read over the report. I'm going to see if I can get the paperwork started on getting a warrant to obtain Stacy Prescott's fingerprints and DNA. She's still our prime suspect."

Scott opened the file with concentrated interest then, eager to study what was in it. He wanted to gather all the information he could, so he could help his partner solve this crime.

* * * *

That evening, Scott had a dinner date with Debbie. Since Debbie lived in Shively, they chose to dine at an O'Charleys on Dixie Highway in that area of town. They sat in the bar area, at one of the six, high, square tables available there. Debbie sat on a high wooden chair, facing a wall and more tables. Scott faced the glass door leading to the bathroom and a large screen television.

Off to the left, Scott could also see a mural on the wall. All O'Charleys had these paintings. This one paid tribute to Louisville and the outlying Shively area. It displayed a Louisville Slugger's bat with Shively written in red through it, Derby roses, the Aegon building from downtown Louisville, and Louisville boxing great Muhammad Ali.

A shiny wooden bar, with several bar stools, graced the side of the dining area. All of the sudden, Debbie caught a glimpse of Chad Kennison's face on one of the televisions above the bar. "Scott, isn't that the murder you are investigating?" she asked, pointing at the TV.

He glanced at the large screen television ahead of him, tuned to the same channel as the smaller televisions in the bar area. Scott answered Debbie's question. "Yes. Why? Do you know that man?"

"Sort of. He was serving jury duty with me. He was quite a playboy," she admitted. Then she coyly confessed, "In fact...he tried to pick me up one day..."

"Well, the fact that he tried to pick you up doesn't surprise me," Scott admitted with an admiring smile. "Any man with a brain and a good set of eyes would want to do that," he complimented. She had her long, straight hair down tonight, so he reached to affectionately run his fingers through a few, soft strands.

"Smooze," Debbie teased, with a radiant grin. "Keep it up. I like it."

"Not smooze. It's the truth," Scott argued, bending to give Debbie an appreciative peck on the lips. "I'm just glad you didn't decide to run off with that handsome, rich guy."

"He was a real player. He had a jealous girlfriend as well. She kind of threatened me in the lobby of the Judicial Center."

"What do you mean by that?" Scott questioned. His playful nature turned to concern on a dime.

"It was nothing major," Debbie assured him, touched by the anxiety she saw in his eyes. "I saw her talking to playboy outside of the Jury Pool Assembly Room. She looked angry. I walked on past and headed down the stairs. I was anxious to meet you outside. The girl followed me downstairs. She came up to me and let it be known that she was Chad's fiancé, and I should stay off her turf if I knew what was good for me. Chad grabbed her by the arm and pulled her away, and I left the building. That was the end of it."

"When did this happen, Debbie?" Scott asked. His detective's mind tuned in now. *If it was Chad's fiancé, it must have been Stacy. And if Chad was philandering... motive for murder, perhaps?*

"Thursday of my first week of jury duty," Debbie answered. "Why? Do you think the girlfriend killed him?" her curious mind caused her to ask.

"She's our prime suspect right now, yes," Scott informed her. "What did the woman you met look like?'"

"She was about five-four, had short, curly, red hair and blue eyes," Debbie described.

"That sounds like Stacy. Chad's fiancé," Scott revealed.

"Oh my gosh! Are you telling me I might have been confronted by a murderer?" Stacy asked with shock.

"It's possible," Scott confirmed.

This thought gave Debbie the creeps. Scott could see the distress in her face. *It's also possible you might have to testify in a murder trial*, he knew, but did not volunteer. He did not want to give Debbie cause for further worry.

Happy with this new information, portraying Stacy as a jealous individual, Scott could not wait to share his news with Roger. *If Stacy threatened Debbie from just a conversation, what might she have done to Chad if she actually caught him in a sex act with another person – a man to boot?* They would have even more reason to obtain a search warrant for Stacy Prescott now. Scott steered his conversation with Debbie in a different direction then, intent on enjoying a relaxing evening with the love of his life.

* * * *

Bright and early the next morning, Scott shared with Roger what he learned from Debbie about Chad Kennison and his jealous, threatening girlfriend. As expected, these facts gave Roger even more reason to seek out a search warrant for Stacy Prescott.

No sooner had they obtained the warrant to collect Stacy's fingerprints and DNA, then the Prescott family attorney, Stuart McClain, contacted them. Roger took the call. When he found out it was Prescott's attorney, he put the call on hold.

"Scott," he called to his partner. Scott looked over at him. "I need to conference you in on a call."

"Okay," Scott agreed without question. He answered the phone as soon as it rang.

"Mr. McClain," Roger addressed the attorney. "I have my partner, Scott Arnold, listening in on the call."

"Fine by me," Stuart McClain answered. "I also have Donald Prescott, Stacy's father conferenced in."

"Mr. Prescott," Roger acknowledged.

"I want to know why you detectives are harassing my daughter," Donald Prescott spoke up.

"We aren't harassing her, sir," Roger defended. "We have collected some evidence from the murder scene that could possibly fit Stacy, or may have nothing at all to do with her. We need her DNA to determine this..."

"Or to help you convict her," Donald argued. "You don't need a DNA sample. My daughter did *not* murder anyone. I can personally vouch for her innocence. The night Chad was murdered, Stacy was home with her mother and me the whole night."

"And you, and your wife, and Stacy were together the whole night," Roger delved a little deeper.

"I didn't have my eye on Stacy constantly, if that's what you are getting at," Donald snapped. "But she didn't leave the house. Her car never left the garage. You need to be focusing your efforts on finding the real killer. Chad Kennison was a fine young man. I was anxious to have him as a son-in-law. He deserves justice."

"And he will get justice," Roger assured him. "If Stacy is innocent, you should have no fear of us doing a DNA test on her," he pointed out.

"Let it go, detective, or you'll find yourself served with a harassment suit. Understand?"

"Yes, sir," Roger replied. "You have a great day," he said with some sarcasm, ending their conversation.

Donald Prescott hung the receiver up with a bang. Stuart McClain further threatened, "You should look to other avenues, detectives. It would make your lives a lot easier."

"We'll look in whatever avenues we need to look in," Roger dug in his heels. "I will talk to you at another time, Mr. McClain."

"I hope that isn't necessary," he gave one final warning. "Good day, detectives."

"Good day to you too," Roger said, adding the word 'prick' under his breath after he disconnected from the call.

Chapter 15

The Plot

The Commonwealth Attorney paid a visit to the Chamberlain Lane lab. The laboratory was dark, dull, and uninspiring inside. The diversity of tests run, coupled with the need for contamination control and evidence management, also produced a collection of segregated spaces rather than a pleasant, cohesive whole. Some of the chemicals used to produce results also left the lab with a strong, unpleasant stench. Darrell sought out and found Mickey Charles – the head of this private lab.

"Hey, Darry," Mickey greeted, looking up from his microscope. He had been analyzing evidence from another homicide. Mickey and Darry had been friends – close as brothers – since college, over twenty years. "What brings you to my world?"

Dressed in a double-breasted, grey, tailored suit and a starched, white shirt, with monogrammed cufflinks and a maroon, silk tie flawlessly knotted around the neck, Darrell stuck out like a sore thumb in the lab atmosphere. Mickey, on the other hand, wore a yellowish white, lab coat. He sported a head full of thick, wavy, black hair. It always looked as if he had not touched a comb to it. Mickey had the perfect look for someone who worked in a lab – the ideal image of a mad professor.

"Can I talk to you in private for a moment?" Darrell asked.

Mickey noticed how serious Darry's face was. "Sure," he agreed without hesitation. Mickey pulled off his plastic gloves and stepped out into the dim, empty hallway with Darrell. "What's up?"

"I need a favor from you, buddy. This one is major," he relayed, placing his right arm around his back and squeezing his shoulder. Darry's large, gold-nugget ring briefly caught Mickey's eye. His nails on both hands were also manicured. *The man's done well for himself.*

"Okay. Tell me what you need, and I'll see what I can do," Mickey pledged.

"You guys are running a DNA analysis for us on some bloody clothes found at Preston and Market which might link to one of our homicides. Some short, red, curly hairs were found at the crime scene, and also on the clothes LMPD detectives confiscated by a dumpster at Preston & Market."

"Yeah. So?"

"These same detectives are searching Stacy Prescott's house today and obtaining DNA samples from her. The DNA will be brought here for testing. I need for the DNA from Stacy's hairs to match to the DNA of the female hairs we already found at the crime scene and on the bloody clothes from beside the dumpster…"

"What?" Mickey asked in shock.

"Stacy is Donald Prescott's daughter. She has become the number one suspect in this murder. I need for her red hair to replace the female ones you have," he repeated. Then he added, "This is our chance to get revenge on Prescott. He raped my sister when we were in college and got off scotch free. But we can make him suffer, through his daughter, now. Can you help me?"

Mickey abhorred Donald Prescott. The man bragged at the frat house, when they were in college, about getting away with date rape. His father's money bought him out of punishment for raping Darry's sister. He would love to see the man suffer. *But can I tamper with evidence and take his daughter down to do it?*

"So can you help me or not?" Darrell pushed. "You know the hell Mary has gone through because of this man. Old Testament says an eye for an eye. I'm all up for that right now. We have a chance to set things right here. What do you say?"

"Darry, I'd love to see Donald Prescott suffer, but tampering with evidence...and taking down his daughter..."

"It's the only way," Darrell argued. "You know you love Mary like a sister. We can avenge her rape. Why should you or I care about Donald Prescott's daughter? He sure didn't care about Mary. Help me out here, buddy," he pleaded.

A forensics investigator for many years, Mickey had a solid reputation to uphold. "Darry, I think you became Commonwealth Attorney because of Mary. To right the wrongs of the world. You've been doing a great job for years. Neither one of us can take the chance of messing up our reputations by doing something stupid. I know you'd like to get even with Donald Prescott, but this isn't the way. I'm sorry, Darry. I can't do what you're asking. I'd give you, or Mary, the shirt off my back. But I won't break the law. As far as I'm concerned, we never had this conversation. Okay?"

Silence reigned for several moments. Darrell wanted to argue his case some more, but he realized it would be no use. He just put Mickey – an honest man – in a very awkward position. "I'm sorry, Mickey. I shouldn't have asked," Darrell said, feeling remorse now.

"It's okay, Darry. I understand. And I would have loved to have helped you."

"I know. Thanks, pal," Darrell said, giving his shoulder one last squeeze before he released him.

Mickey watched Darry walk away. A tall man, he hunched over, as if he bore heavy weight upon his shoulders. Hearing Donald Prescott's name again brought back all the pain for Mary. Mickey was tempted to change his mind and help Darry, but he knew he could not do it. *Donald Prescott will get his some day, even if we have to wait until the son of a bitch burns in hell.*

Mickey's heart was heavy. Difficult doing the right thing, he knew he must. He lumbered back into the lab.

Chapter 16

Stacy's DNA

Christopher Hughes joined Roger and Scott on their search of the Prescott home. His role was to gather the DNA and fingerprint samples. He would then take charge of this possible evidence and send it on its way to the lab.

This time, the DNA would not be going to Frankfort. They were sending these samples to the private lab on Chamberlain Lane again, because Roger and Scott wanted a faster turnaround time. They needed ready answers as to whether Stacy Prescott's DNA matched to the DNA from the Kennison crime scene.

When the three investigators arrived at the Prescott home, another immense home in Lake Forest, Stuart McClain greeted them. "Stuart, are you living with the Prescotts now?" Roger asked. He turned to Christopher and told him, "This is Stuart McClain, the Prescott attorney."

"Oh," Christopher replied. His disliked the man just by learning this knowledge.

Christopher took a second to give him a thorough perusal. Dressed in an expensive, pinstriped, tailored suit, and polished, unblemished, black shoes, he also had on a pale blue shirt with a stiff white collar and gold – *I'm sure they are real gold* – monogrammed cufflinks. A satin, navy tie hung from his neck.

Clean-shaven, his face so smooth it almost shone, his short, black hair impeccable, this man embodied perfection. His deep-set, dark brown eyes imposed a sense of fear. *I bet Prescott pays him big bucks to cover his butt.*

In radical contrast, Roger donned his usual, crumpled, polyester blend suit, and Christopher's hair had a wet, spiked look. "I guess you already know why we are here," Roger said, pulling forth the warrant.

"Yes. That's why I'm here," he told them.

Apparent there was a leak within their department; Stuart had been notified they were about to do this search. Roger did not care whether Stuart was there or not. Stuart could not stop them from gathering evidence. He could only keep Stacy from talking to them and making a confession.

"I'm going to make sure you don't abuse any privileges," Stuart enlightened them. Then he went on to insult, "This whole thing is ludicrous, and it's a shame a killer is free to roam the streets while you investigate a family that is beyond reproach."

Yeah, right! Christopher mused with age-old resentment. Coming from a working-class family, he did not care much for the elites of society. He fought to keep from rolling his eyes at this man.

"Well, enough with the pleasantries," Roger said in a voice laced with sarcasm. "We have a warrant to search this house and collect DNA and fingerprint samples from Stacy Prescott. We'd like to get started."

Stuart stepped back and allowed the three of them to enter. "Stacy is in the great room," he told them.

"Okay. We'll go to the great room first then," Roger agreed.

Stuart led them through the long entrance foyer. He took them into a vast room with a high, post and beam cathedral ceiling and a polished, natural wood floor. Sitting on a wraparound, leather sofa in the middle of the room, Stacy stared straight ahead. She had her palms crossed in her lap, fidgeting with them. The corners of her mouth turned downward; her eyes screamed melancholy.

"Stacy, these men are going to gather some DNA and fingerprint samples from you. You need say nothing to them. Just do as they ask," Stuart instructed her.

She nodded. Christopher approached her. He pulled on rubber gloves and extracted a comb from his tackle box evidence carrier. "I need to comb through your hair a bit. I'm going to gather some hair samples from you," he explained.

"Okay," she uttered in a small voice. She did not look him in the face. Instead, she looked over his shoulder, out the wall of glass windows looking out into the yard.

Christopher carefully ran the comb through a section of her hair. He could feel Stacy tremble. *She's scared. I wonder why, if she is innocent*, he pondered. He gathered the hairs from the comb and sealed them in a plastic bag. He marked something on the bag and then placed it in his evidence case.

Next, Christopher pulled forth a cotton swab. "I need for you to open your mouth."

Stacy did not say anything this time. She merely opened her mouth and waited. Christopher very gently swabbed the side of her cheek a few times. He dropped the cotton swab into a container, sealed it, and wrote something on the outside of this item as well. Then he also stashed it in his case.

Lastly, Christopher set up the fingerprinting kit on the coffee table in front of Stacy. He made inked prints of each of Stacy's fingers. He also cautiously preserved these samples. "That's all I need. Thank you," he said, being polite.

Stacy silently nodded again.

"Now, if you can show us to the kitchen, that would be grand," Roger said to Stuart.

"Stacy, you wait here. I'll be back when they are through," Stuart instructed the girl before he left the room with the detectives.

"Okay," she muttered. She looked close to tears.

Gleaming, gigantic appliances – a side-by-side refrigerator, a range and oven, a dishwasher, and a good-sized, built-in microwave – met them in the massive kitchen. A butcher block, with pots and pans decoratively hanging overhead, stood in the center of the room. In the middle of the butcher block sat a knife block, with two knives missing from it. The detectives checked the dishwasher, but they found no sign of the knives. They confiscated the whole knife block as possible evidence.

They moved on to Stacy's bedroom next. This room contained a queen-sized, canopied bed. The sheer, floral, swooped fabric hanging from the valance at the top of the two sizeable windows matched perfectly to the material adorning the bed.

The detectives made their way over to a huge walk-in closet. Stepping inside, they soon discovered several empty shoeboxes. Another lucky break in the case, the brand name on one of the empty shoeboxes matched to the pair of shoes found in the alley.

They left the Prescott residence feeling satisfied with their search. Stuart McClain tried to rain on their parade as he let them out of the house. "Well, I hope you are happy with your useless search. Now, maybe you can prove Stacy's innocence and move on, as you should have already been doing."

"We'll be in touch," Roger promised him with a smug smile.

Stuart shut the door with a bang almost as soon as the detectives cleared the doorway. "Christopher, we look forward to hearing back from the lab soon," Roger told him before they all got into their cars and headed off.

"I'll drop it by there today, and they'll get back with you as soon as possible," Christopher promised. He wondered if Stacy did have something to do with this murder now. Prescott's attorney seemed very nervous as well.

* * * *

Working in the lab, as usual, Mickey Charles received a phone call. "Chamberlain Lane Lab. Mickey Charles speaking," he answered.

"Mr. Charles," a man's voice addressed him. "This is Stuart McClain, Stacy Prescott's attorney."

"What can I do for you, Mr. McClain?" Mickey asked, giving the call his full attention. He had still been working on preparing some evidence for analysis. Test tubes and slides resided on the long counter in front of him. A telescope, computer and other useful machines sat atop the table as well.

"Well, it's not what you can do for me, Mr. Charles. It's what you can do for the Prescott family. Donald Prescott would very much appreciate it if you would be very careful with your findings in his daughter's case. He tells me you were an old frat brother of his. He knows you have lost touch during the years, but he was wondering if perhaps you might like to come out to the country club. He could see to it you are made a member. Then you could use the gym, swimming pool and everything whenever you'd like. He also could see to it that any other expenses you might entail there; food, drinks, etc., were covered by him as well. For yourself, or even you and a date. He wants to show his gratitude to you for helping his daughter."

"Are you offering me a bribe?" Mickey asked, striping off his goggles as if he could see through the phone line. He would have been incredulous had this been anyone but Donald Prescott.

"No. No, of course not. I'm just telling you Donald would like to renew old ties, and you know how the saying goes, 'You scratch his back, and he'll scratch yours'."

"Uh-huh," Mickey responded. He had a death grip on the receiver now. "Well, you tell Mr. Prescott if his daughter isn't guilty, he has nothing to worry about. And if she is, he can sink all his money on your expenses and trying to buy her innocence. The same way as some slick attorney once bought his."

"Mr. Charles, I'm not sure I like what you are implying," Stuart said.

"Yeah, well, I don't like the bribe you just implied either, Mr. McClain. You just tell Mr. Prescott I will do my job to the best of my ability, and justice will be served. Got that?"

"I've got that loud and clear," Stuart replied. "If you change your mind, feel free to give me a call back."

"Don't hold your breath," Mickey snapped. He lowered the phone receiver with a clatter,   seething. He could not believe Donald Prescott just had his attorney try to bribe him. *But then again, why shouldn't I? The man is slime! He always has been. And if they are this worried about Stacy, could the apple fall far from the tree?*

He suddenly wished all the evidence would match to Stacy. He would like to see her suffer. Even though Donald would throw all of his money into defending her, Mickey would enjoy seeing him sweat.

An image of Mary floated through his mind. Such an innocent girl, Donald took full advantage of her. He stole her innocence and ruined her life, and walked away without punishment, laughing about it. Mickey desired to make Donald pay. All at once, Darry's request, to tamper with evidence and make sure it matched, looked better and better. Mickey fought his rage as he snapped his goggles back in place and attempted to focus on the business at hand once more.

* * * *

Another month passed before Roger and Scott got back the results from the Chamberlain Lane lab. "Bingo!" Roger exclaimed. He read through the results on the items from Preston and Market and the fingerprinting and DNA testing for Stacy Prescott.

"What is it?" Scott asked, walking over to Roger's desk.

"We may have gotten our break," Roger said, handing him the file.

Scott took a second to read over the report. "I'll say," he agreed with a smile. It looks like the fingerprints on Chad's shoulder are a direct match to Stacy Prescott's fingerprints. It also says the blood DNA on the clothes found by the dumpster matches to Chad, and the DNA in the female, red hairs, both at the murder site and on the clothes found by the dumpster, all match to Stacy Prescott," Scott pointed out with a smile.

"The fingerprint matches are nice. But this evidence doesn't matter as much as the DNA match. We have her cold there. We need to get a warrant for Stacy Prescott's arrest. I need to call Darrell Adams and share all this with him. I think we've done a bang up job of filling in the blanks on this crime, rookie."

"I guess," Scott said under his breath. Roger had already picked up the phone to call Darrell, so he was no longer paying any attention to Scott.

Scott walked back over to his desk still studying the Forensics file. *I wish we knew who the male suspect was that was giving Chad a blowjob that night. I'd like to be certain they did not have anything to do with this murder.* This missing piece of the puzzle bothered him a great deal. Scott did not like leaving loose ends in his cases.

Once again, as in his first case, Renee Peterson's suicide, irritating worries lingered in the back of his mind. *Will I have these with every case*, he wondered. *I guess none of the cases will be cut and dried*, he tried to assure himself. But he could not seem to make himself put down the Forensics file.

* * * *

Darrell Adams and Mickey Charles met for a drink in a small, out of the way, bar. They sat at a small table in a dark corner by themselves. There were not many patrons anyway, and the others who were there were sitting at the bar. "Mickey, what gives?" Darrell got right to the point.

"What do you mean, what gives?" Mickey answered with a question. "What gives is the DNA and fingerprint samples from Stacy matched DNA and fingerprints found at the crime scene. They also match the hairs discovered on the clothing found at Preston and Market *now* as well. I hope Stacy burns in hell, and it tears her daddy's heart out," Mickey stated with wrath.

"So is this just dumb luck, or did you make any changes?" Darrell dared to ask.

"Some of her hairs *were* found at the crime scene. As to the hairs on the clothes from Preston and Market, let's just say...for Mary. Shall we?" Mickey answer was purposely vague. He raised his drink – a shot of tequila – and drained it down his throat.

"For Mary," Darrell agreed, raising his beer bottle and tapping it to Mickey's empty shot glass. He also gave his friend a pat on his upper arm. "I owe you, buddy. Big time."

"You owe me nothing, Darry," Mickey replied. "I'm just helping see justice is done once and for all. Donald Prescott deserves to pay."

Nothing more was said about this case. In fact, Darrell was determined that nothing more would ever be said. Stacy Prescott was guilty, and they had the evidence to prove it. He would seek a homicide indictment against Stacy Prescott from the Grand Jury. Then he would have a warrant for her arrest issued. He intended to do his damnedest to see she was punished to the full extent of the law. *An eye for an eye.*

Chapter 17

Juror Number 185

Tuesday, nearing four o'clock, Scott called Debbie's cell phone, for the fourth time – no answer. He had not heard a word from her all day. Normally, they talked several times a day. He was unsettled.

Debbie usually had her cell phone turned on and answered right away. *Wonder if she's in court today*, he speculated. Normally if she was in court representing a child's rights, then she called and told him.

As it neared 5:00 p.m., Scott decided to call CASA and see if they might know where Debbie was. "CASA of Jefferson County. Marla speaking. Can I help you?" a woman answered.

"Hi, Marla. It's detective Scott Arnold," he replied.

"Can I help you with something, Detective Arnold?" she asked.

"Well…I'm hoping someone can," he replied. "I'm calling on a personal matter."

"A personal matter?"

"Yes. My girlfriend, Debbie Gray, works there. I haven't been able to reach her all day. And I was wondering if you, or someone else there, can tell me if she is tied up in court with some child's case."

"Let me check for you," the woman offered. She placed Scott on hold for a few minutes. Then another woman picked up the call. "Detective Arnold, this is Maryann," she told him.

Scott knew who Maryann was. He had heard Debbie talk of her. "Hi, Maryann," he said. "I've heard a lot about you from Debbie. I'm Scott, Debbie's boyfriend."

"Yes. She has talked about you as well," she revealed with a carefree chuckle. "I'm a bit worried about Debbie, Scott," she admitted.

"Why?" she asked.

"She is AWOL today," she informed him.

"AWOL?" he repeated.

"Yes. She didn't show up today. I've tried to contact her at home, but I've gotten no answer."

Now Scott was concerned. This was not like Debbie at all. If for some reason she could not make it to work, she would have called.

"Okay. Thanks for the information, Maryann. I need to find out what's up," he said both to her and to himself.

"Well, when you track her down, if she can't make it in again tomorrow, tell her to be sure and call," Maryann instructed.

"I sure will," Scott assured her. He thanked her again, and then he hung up.

Very worried about Debbie, he rashly decided, *I need to go to Debbie's house and find out what's up.* He needed to get to the bottom of things before he could concentrate on work anymore.

* * * *

When Scott pulled into Debbie's driveway, he discovered her car parked there. *Well, it seems like she's home,* he concluded. *I wonder if she's sick,* he thought with anxiety.

If she was sick enough she did not even call the CASA, or him, he felt he had reason for concern.

Scott got out of his car, walked up to the front door, knocked, and rang the bell. He waited. After several minutes passed without any response, he knocked a little louder and rang the bell with persistence – still no response.

"Shit!" he cursed, raking a hand through his hair. He also tapped one of his feet.

Debbie's bedroom was in the back of the house. *If she's ill, she's likely in bed. Should I go around back and peek in the window. Something's definitely wrong. Debbie's not that heavy of a sleeper. If she's in the house, she should have heard me knocking and ringing the bell.*

Scott made his way off the porch, up the driveway, and through the back gate. He walked across the back of the house. Debbie's bedroom was on the far end of the house. Scott stepped inside a stone border, cautiously trying not to step on anything in Debbie's flower garden. He made his way up to Debbie's bedroom window. He drew in close to the glass, cupped his hands beside his eyes, and pressed them to the window.

He could see Debbie's bed. Her bed looked un-slept in. The bedspread and lace-trimmed pillows looked undisturbed. *Where the hell could she be?* Scott wondered in trepidation. *If there was some family emergency and she had to go somewhere, she would have called. And someone had to have picked her up, because her car's in the driveway.*

Getting more and more out of sorts, he wanted answers, and he wanted them *now*. Scott hopped out of the flower garden and scurried up the concrete, back porch steps. Mini-blinds in the back door glass concealed his view. He walked along the small deck and made his way over to the kitchen window.

A cloudy day, not a lot of natural light in the house, and the light in the kitchen was not turned on. The kitchen window also sported mini-blinds, but they were pulled up a bit, so the bottom pane was unobstructed. When Scott pressed his face close to the glass this time, he saw Debbie, lying on her side in the floor.

"Oh, crap!" he cursed. They talked about exchanging keys to their houses, but they had not done so yet. *I've got to get inside*, he concluded.

Scott reached down and took off one of his shoes. He also took off his suit jacket and wrapped it around his hand and wrist. He aimed the steel heel of his shoe toward the bottom pane of glass in the back door and struck it with slight force. The glass shattered and fell in the inside floor with a clatter. He knocked other jagged pieces out of the way before he placed his wadded up suit jacket in the broken frame to shelter his arm from any other stray pieces of glass. He reached to unlock the back door.

Scott turned the doorknob and sent the door flying open. He rushed toward Debbie's side. He wrenched to a stop, when he saw all of the blood around her body. He also noted her hands were handcuffed behind her back. "Damn! Dammit!" he swore.

Instinct told him to drop to his knees and cradle Debbie's body, but his police training told him otherwise. The amount of blood present divulged Debbie's death. Regardless, Scott felt an overwhelming need to check for a pulse.

As Scott stooped behind Debbie back, he observed a gaping wound across her throat. *Just like Chad Kennison. Debbie's throat's been slit*, he observed. Bile rose in his throat; his chest constricted. Scott placed his fingers just above the womb in Debbie's neck to check for a pulse. *No pulse*. His last hope extinguished.

Scott's eyes moved further along Debbie's body. A knife handle protruding from between Debbie's legs rattled him so much he lost his balance. He staggered forward, clumsily falling over the top of Debbie's body. His hands caught his fall, hitting the tile floor hard, and landing, palm down, in Debbie's blood. Her blood splattered upward on the bottom of his shirt sleeves.

"Son of a bitch!" he continued to swear. His chest throbbed as if he had been the one stabbed – right through the heart. *My God! What have I let happen? Could Stacy have done this?*

As Scott struggled to straighten back up, he was startled by a loud command, "Freeze! Raise your hands in the air where I can see them."

He raised his blood-soaked hands high in the air and looked over his shoulder. As suspected, a police officer stood just inside the kitchen. The officer's gun drawn; it pointed right at Scott. *My God! It looks like* I've *done this!*

"I'm an LMPD detective," Scott announced. "My badge is in my wallet. Right back pocket."

The police officer slowly approached Scott. Another officer right behind him also had his gun drawn on Scott. The first officer extracted Scott's wallet and opened it. Once he saw the badge, he holstered his gun and directed the other officer to do the same.

"I'm sorry, detective," he apologized. "A neighbor called to say there was a prowler looking in back windows. I was en-route when they called back to say you broke out glass in the back door. Is this true? What's up? Were you making an arrest?" He stared at the handcuffed victim and Scott's bloody hands.

"I'll explain it all to you in a moment," Scott replied. "Right now, I need for you to call in Shively's homicide investigators and Metro's. I believe this murder is tied to another we are working on. The MO's exactly the same."

"Why'd you contaminate the crime scene?" the other, young, police officer asked, also fixated on Scott's bloodstained hands.

"It was an accident," Scott claimed. "Can we please just call in the homicide teams and get the ball rolling on this investigation?"

Scott's mind still could not wrap itself around Debbie's death and mutilation. No emotional attachment existed in investigating the death of strangers. *Finding someone you love is a whole other thing.* His legs shook; his stomach churned; his head pounded; he even found it hard to breathe.

Glancing at his blood-spattered hands and shirtsleeves one last time, Scott secretly pledged, *I'll find out who did this, and when I do, I'll make them pay.*

* * * *

On the scene, from the LMPD Homicide Squad, Christopher Hughes arrived first. Roger walked in next, and the coroner, Matt Smith, came last.

Roger pulled Scott aside, at once. "You need to head to the station now, rookie," he instructed.

"What? No. I want to be involved in this investigation," Scott argued. "The MO's the same as Chad Kennison. It could have been Stacy. You know she threatened Debbie once."

He wiped the blood from his hands, at last, with a wet paper towel. Christopher took photographs of his bloody hands and sleeves before Shively detectives would allow him to clean up. Part of the evidence in this case now, Scott understood he was a suspect.

"You're already *are* involved in this investigation. And not in a good way. You broke in the house, and you contaminated the murder site. You should have called in Shively Police to assist. Now, *you* are a suspect in this homicide."

"Don't get crazy on me, Roger," Scott demanded. "Debbie was my girlfriend...the love of my life." His voice broke, and Scott struggled to continue. "You know I was planning to propose to her. I told you this. There is no way I would ever harm a hair on her head. But I want to be assigned to this case, so I can track down Stacy, or whoever did this, and make them pay."

"You've already done two stupid things. You're too personally involved to be any good to this case. You are through with this investigation, Scott. Another team will investigate, and I'll supervise. Besides, the Public Integrity Unit will want to talk to you when you get back to the station, since you broke protocol and broke into the victim's house."

"Roger, I don't have time for this bullshit," Scott bickered.

"Well, you are going to make time. I want you to leave and head to the station now. I'll gather the facts here, and I'll let you know what we've found once you are cleared as a suspect by the Public Integrity Unit. Now scram!"

Scott's hands balled and his posture and face rigid, his pain physically showed. Roger felt for him. He would have liked to have let him stay, but he did not believe Scott could be objective on this case. Scott would have to take a backseat to someone else, whether he liked it or not.

Roger understood why Scott did what he had, and even with all of his years of experience, he might have done likewise. But Roger needed to follow protocol, and doing so meant Scott needed to report to the Public Integrity Unit. He cared enough about Scott that he would not let him risk throwing away his career by not following protocol.

"Bye, Scott," Roger dismissed him. He walked over to talk with Matt Smith instead.

Scott stood there for a moment longer. Then he turned and stormed out of the house. He would follow protocol for now. But the department would not keep him from investigating Debbie's murder and bringing her murderer to justice. Her death would not go un-avenged.

Chapter 18

The Confession

Having finished being raked over the coals by the Public Integrity Unit, Scott heard Stacy Prescott was in the interrogation room with Roger. She had voluntarily come in. He headed straight there.

Without invite, Scott opened the door to the interrogation room and entered. Roger looked up when he heard the door open. When he saw Scott enter, he arose from his chair. "Excuse me one moment," he said to Stacy.

He approached Scott, who still stood near the doorway. "What are you doing here?" he asked him in a voice barely above a whisper.

"I have some questions I need answers to," Scott answered. "I think maybe Stacy can answer them."

"Maybe. Maybe not," Roger answered. He was clutching Scott's upper arm now. "Let's step outside for a moment and we'll discuss this matter."

"I don't want to step outside," Scott quarreled, raising his voice a bit.

"Too bad," Roger held his ground, gritting his teeth.

"Is there a problem?" Stacy asked. She eyeballed Scott with an intent stare.

"No. There isn't," Scott stubbornly proclaimed. He shook loose from Roger's grasp and approached the table. "I have a few questions for you, Stacy."

"O...okay," she answered a little unsurely. She looked oddly at the blood stains on the end of Scott's shirt now.

"Fine," Scott said. He pulled out a chair and sat down across from her.

Seething, Roger begrudgingly walked back over to the table as well, sitting between the two of them. Scott was determined to be there, and Roger understood why. He would allow him to stay in the room and ask some questions, but he intended to keep a close eye on him. And he would stop him and forcefully eject him from the room if Scott got out of hand. Already in enough trouble right now, Roger did not want to see Scott jeopardize his career due to grief.

"So what are your questions?" Stacy asked.

"Stacy, were you at the Judicial Center the first Thursday that Chad was serving jury duty?"

"Th...ursday?" she repeated. "What does the Thursday before Chad's murder have to do with anything?"

"He was murdered Friday, right?" Scott confirmed. "So why would you have a problem discussing something that happened on Thursday?"

"I...I guess I don't..." she replied, glancing at Roger as if she expected him to clear up the confusion. Scott looked angry and mean, and he scared her a bit. She wondered if she made the right decision in coming here.

Scott wanted to reach across the table and throttle Stacy. She seemed deliberately evasive. And he wanted answers, not stalling. *Is she trying to hide her guilt?*

"Well...let me put it to you this way, Stacy..." Scott said, breathing fire. "I can get a simple answer from you to this question, or I can have my girlfriend identify you. She believes the two of you talked at the Judicial Center that particular Thursday. Chad was talking to my girlfriend first, and evidently it bothered you a bit. You had a few heated words with my girlfriend," Scott added, staring holes through Stacy.

Scott wanted to see how she reacted to this data. Stacy looked distressed. *Why's she worried? If she's Debbie's murderer, she knows she is dead and can't identify her. Or is she upset because she fears Debbie is still alive, after she tried to kill her, and* can *identify her?*

"What are you trying to get at?" she questioned with confusion. "If you are trying to make the case that I perhaps murdered Chad because I was jealous and afraid he was involved with your girlfriend, I'd have to argue that you would have as much motive to have murdered Chad as I did. Maybe you should be the one sitting here being questioned. Now there's a thought."

Just as cutting off your air supply until you die is, Scott thought with fury. He contained his rage and said, "I don't have to make a case against you, Stacy. Your DNA, found at the scene of Chad's murder, is already doing that. If you don't want to answer any questions here, that's fine. You can do so at your murder trial. I'll be sure and testify you refused to answer our questions. Don't you think the jury might find that odd? Almost makes it seem you were trying to hide something, doesn't it?"

"I can't stand this!" Stacy exclaimed. "I loved Chad. I didn't kill him," she professed. "But, yes, I was at the Judicial Center on that Thursday, and I did have words with some woman there about coming on to Scott. If she is your girlfriend, detective, you might want to keep a close eye on her, because she seemed to have the hots for Chad."

Keep a close eye on her...as if she is still alive? Is Stacy just toying with me, or does she not know Debbie is dead?

"I might do that, but you see, that would be impossible. Do you know why?"

Stacy looked confused. "Why?" she asked, taking the bait.

"Because my girlfriend was found dead today. Her throat slit and her genitals mutilated, just like Chad. So where exactly were you last night, Stacy?"

Fixated on Stacy's reaction to his news about Debbie, Scott watched her mouth drop open, her eyes round, and the color drain from her face. "I didn't kill anyone," she shrieked, bursting into tears. "But...I...I did see Chad dead... That's why I came here today...to tell the truth."

Hanging on the end of his seat, Scott hoped, *Are we about to have a confession here?* "Tell us, Stacy," Scott encouraged. "We need to hear the truth from you."

"I went down to the Judicial Center again Friday afternoon. I hung around outside for several hours waiting for Chad. He was supposed to call me when he was through for the day. He didn't know I was waiting for him outside."

Stacy paused and took a deep breath. Then she continued, "Chad finally called, said he had been interviewed to be on a jury, but hadn't been chosen. He said he was leaving. This was about 6:45 p.m. He said he was going to get some dinner and go home. I waited around, off to the side of the Judicial Center, and watched for him to come out. He came out with the some woman I had never seen before. She had her arm linked with his, and they looked very chummy. I followed them to the parking garage on the corner. My car was parked there too. We lucked into being on the same floor. I followed Scott, at a distance, after we drove out of the garage. They went to the Petrus Restaurant and Nightclub on Main. I saw him park his car by the building. I circled the block and parked in the parking garage on the corner."

"So did you go into Petrus and confront Chad and this chummy, unknown woman?" Scott asked.

"No. I paid one of the bouncers to keep an eye on Chad and to let me know when they left. I figured they would only be there about an hour or so. I went into the nightclub and hung out, waiting. The restaurant is on the first floor, and the nightclub is on the second. It doesn't officially open until 10:00, so I had the whole place all to myself. They wouldn't let just anyone go into the nightclub and wait like this, but Chad and I are VIP members of Petrus," she informed Scott, sounding proud of her prestige.

"And?" Scott prodded her on.

"And...Chad and this woman were in the restaurant an hour and a half. But, about 8:30, instead of leaving, Chad took this woman upstairs to the VIP floor. I saw them pass on the stairs; the VIP floor is a floor above the nightclub. Chad did not see me. He had his face buried in this woman's hair, practically pushing her up the stairs. The VIP floor isn't supposed to open until 10:00 either, but I wasn't the only one paying for extra privileges."

"So did you follow them up there?"

"No. I went downstairs to talk to the bouncer, and he told me Chad slipped him a few dollars to let him and this woman go up early, as I assumed. He also said they purchased a bottle of wine from the restaurant bar and taken it and two glasses upstairs with them. The restaurant has a huge, fully stocked bar. The VIP floor has a smaller, private bar, but it would not open until 10:00. So they had a bottle of wine and the entire VIP floor to themselves. It's a cozy floor, with leather loveseats and cloth wraparound chairs. Chad and this woman were on that floor for two hours – an hour and a half of that all by themselves. I can only imagine what all they might have been doing." Stacy paused for a second then, a pained expression on her face. She contemplated what they had likely been doing.

Scott verified, "So they came off the VIP floor about...uh...10:30? Is this correct?"

"Yeah. I glanced at my watch when I saw them *finally* come into the nightclub. It *was* about 10:30. A pretty good-sized crowd was already in the club. Friday nights at Petrus the nightclub gets overrun. There's a live band, an ample bar, with saltwater aquariums built in all around it, and a huge, mirrored dance floor. I sat at a small table in a dark corner, and I watched Chad and this woman stand by the bar drinking, flirting, and touching. A private, small table at the other end of the room eventually opened up. Chad took this woman by the hand and led her to that table. They sat there for a good while, drinking, kissing and cuddling." Stacy took a breather again and looked Scott in the eyes. The hurt in her eyes begged for his empathy.

Scott refused to take the bait. He needed Stacy to continue her crucial narrative. So he asked in an unemotional voice, "So what time did they leave the club?"

"They left about 12:30. After sharing several, intimate dances on the dance floor, as the band moved into their slow set."

"And did you follow them out and confront them then?" Scott questioned.

"I followed them out, and I...I saw... It looked like the woman was giving Scott a blowjob in the alley. My heart broke. It hurt enough to watch them kissing, cuddling and fondling in the restaurant. But now Chad had taken things to a whole new level. He was supposed to be my fiancé. He was supposed to be faithful to me...but...he was having sex with this other woman."

"I bet this made you angry," Scott suggested.

"It did make me mad…"

"Mad…How about furious? So furious you wanted to kill, maybe?" he hypothesized.

Impressed by Scott's line of questioning, Roger saw no reason not to allow him to proceed. Scott appeared to be getting somewhere. They might soon have a confession from Stacy Prescott.

"I wasn't furious at that point," she continued. "Instead, like I said, my heart was breaking. I was shattered. I started crying, so I went back inside Petrus. I went inside the bathroom, went in a stall, sat on a toilet, put my head in my hands, and cried my heart out. When I cried all the tears I could cry, I decided to get out of there. It was 1:00 a.m. As I came out of the club, I glanced down the alley again. I thought I saw someone kneeling in the spot where I had seen Chad and his new woman friend. I should have just kept walking. Instead, I thought maybe Chad collapsed there after his rapture and drinking. He was good about falling asleep right after sex. This is the point where I got furious…as you put it. I decided to march down that alley and throw my engagement ring in his face."

She stopped again then, and her body shuddered. With a horrified expression on her face, she recounted in a faraway voice, "As I got close to his body, I stepped in something wet and sticky. I noticed it was all over the ground around Chad. I called his name, but he didn't respond. I stooped down and grabbed his shoulder to give him a shake. He wouldn't even raise his head. I reached out to raise it for him, and my finger sank inside his throat. I jerked my hand away, breaking one of my nails. It was then I realized I was standing in his blood. I panicked. I should have called the police, but I was afraid they would think I murdered him. I ran behind the building, kicked off my shoes, and I ran. I went inside the parking garage, jumped in my car, and took off. As I drove away, I must have thought about calling the police a million times."

As she looked Scott directly in the eyes, she admitted with a saddened expression, "I haven't been able to get the image of Chad's dead body out of my mind since. I can't even sleep at night. It keeps coming to me in nightmares. But I didn't kill him. He was dead when I got there. I swear. And whoever killed Chad might have killed your girlfriend. You asked where I was last night. I was at school from seven to nine. Then I was home the rest of the evening."

"Is there anyone who can confirm this?" Scott asked.

"There were several hundred people in class with me. U of L's Business Ethics. And my mom and dad can vouch for me being home."

"Just like they did the night of Chad's death? Your father said you were home all evening, and now you are telling us you were gone all that time. His alibi for you doesn't seem very credible to me. What do you think?"

"I'm sorry my father lied. I didn't ask him to do that. Just like my attorney's been telling me to keep quiet. I haven't wanted any of it," she proclaimed. Looking back at Scott, she said, "All I wanted to do was tell the truth. And now I have. You've got the wrong person. You need to track down the real killer, because what they are doing is brutal and sick. No one deserves to die like that, not...not even Chad." She placed her hand over her mouth, closed her eyes, and shook her head after she uttered this last statement. It was as if she was trying to block out awful images from her mind.

"So what did this other woman, who was with Chad before he died, look like?" Scott continued to interrogate, ignoring her emotional state.

Stacy looked back up at Scott, with tears in her eyes. She slipped the hand down from her mouth and revealed,

"She...she looked a lot like me. She was a little taller than I am. But she had short, curly, red hair like mine."

This description fit with the evidence. Except DNA evidence pointed to a man as Chad's sexual partner that night. *Could he have thought he was with a woman? A man in drag, maybe?* Chad may not have been gay as they originally thought.

"Can you remember what this woman was wearing?" Scott dug a little deeper.

"She had on a royal blue, thin, spring sweater, navy slacks and navy flats. And she also had on white evening gloves. I thought this was a little strange," Stacy confessed. "But maybe not if she killed Chad. She was the last person to see him alive that I know of."

The description of the clothes and the white gloves matched to the items found in the garbage bag – items with Chad's blood on them. The murder weapon had also been found amongst these items.

Could this be true? Was the other person the one wearing the clothes, splattered with Chad's blood? Or was Stacy concocting this story to cover her own guilt? If this other person was wearing these clothes, and not Stacy, how did Stacy's hairs get on the clothes?

"Are you sure these weren't the clothes you had on that night instead? You belong to the country club, right? Don't you occasionally wear evening gloves?" Scott probed.

"Yes...but those *weren't* my clothes. I've told you all I know."

"Then how did your hair get on these clothes? You said you didn't confront, or were around, this woman, right?" Scott continued to interrogate, despite Stacy's continued proclamations of her innocence.

"I wasn't," Stacy maintained. "There must be some mistake about my hair," she argued.

"Are you sure these weren't your clothes, and you took them off like you did your shoes? They had Chad's blood on them just like your shoes? When you went downtown to wait for Chad, did you take a knife with you? Were you looking to confront Chad and some woman that evening, Stacy?"

"No!" she protested. "That isn't what happened!" she staunchly upheld.

"You've lied to us once, Stacy, saying you were home when Chad was murdered. How do I know you aren't lying about the clothes as well?" Scott suggested.

"I told you all I know. I would have never hurt Chad," Stacy proclaimed one final time. "I have nothing further to say," Stacy professed. Her eyes looked wounded. They stared at Scott as if he betrayed her.

Their interrogation with Stacy had ended. They had not gotten a confession, and Scott now had worrisome doubts in the back of his mind again. *Who and where was this other person? And what role did they play in Chad's murder?*

Scott debated if Stacy really was the killer. *We need to find this other person. I need to make sure the right person pays for these crimes – if Chad's and Debbie's murders are indeed connected.*

Already planning his next step, Scott decided to go over to the Judicial Center. Debbie told him Chad talked to and tried to pick up several women in the jury pool waiting room. She had only been one of his many targets. *Did the other person in the alley come from there? If so, they might have been serving jury duty as well.* He would search there first. They needed to find this other person. Scott needed clear answers in this case. He needed to find out who killed Debbie and make them pay.

133

Chapter 19

Handcuffs

After Stacy left police headquarters, as Roger and Scott settled back in at their desks, Roger took a second to praise Scott on his detective work. "That was a good interrogation, rookie," he told him.

"If it was so good, then why didn't I get a confession?" Scott asked him, sounding dejected.

"Getting someone to confess to murder is very tough," Roger shared. "But you gathered a lot of great facts. You didn't get Stacy to confess to Chad's murder, but she did confess to being with him in the alley that night. This, combined with the DNA evidence we have, will likely get us a Grand Jury indictment against Stacy. Good job, rookie!" he praised again. He figured Scott could use some positive reinforcement for a change.

"Does this mean I'm back on the case?" Scott pushed, giving Roger a hard stare.

Roger took a second to answer. "We'll see," he said, breaking eye contact. He refused to make any promises to Scott. He did not want to see him get in over his head. Scott still needed to be cleared by the Public Integrity Unit for one thing. "Are you even supposed to still be here today?" Roger suggested.

"The Public Integrity Unit suggested I go home for the rest of the day," Scott revealed.

"Well, then I'd suggest that's what you do. Don't push things with them, Scott. I'm sure you'll be cleared fairly quickly. If you want to be part of this investigation – and I know you do – then you need to play by their rules. Then you can work the case."

Scott pushed his desk chair back and stood up. "Guess I'll get out of here then."

"I'll see you, rookie," Roger said, and began looking at his computer screen.

Scott left the building. Roger thought he was going home, but Scott paid a visit to the Judicial Center instead. Work was good for him right now. He did not want to go home and be alone with his thoughts of Debbie.

As he walked through the metal detectors, he glimpsed Deputy Jack Jordan. Actually, Deputy Jordan's handcuffs caught, and held, Scott's attention.

"Is there something wrong, detective?" Jack asked, noting Scott had stopped and now stared at his waist.

Scott drew closer. He reached to raise the handcuffs, studying the engraving on the side. "These…these are your handcuffs?"

"Yeah. Why?" Jack asked in bewilderment. "Did you lose a pair or something? I engrave mine with my initials – JCJ, Jackson Charles Jordan."

"Yeah. I see that," Scott strangely commented. He released his hold on the handcuffs. The engraved JCJ found on the handcuffs on Renee's ankles matched the engraving on Jack's handcuffs. Scott's mind, all at once, focused on the death of Renee Peterson once more. *But how could those handcuffs have been* his? Scott looked up at Deputy Jordan's face. He found himself studying his orange, wavy hair.

"Detective, are you alright?" Jack asked with concern. This younger man looked as if he lost his senses, standing there mute, eyeballing him.

"Yeah. I'm fine," Scott replied, forcing his eyes to look away. "I'm sorry," he apologized. "It's been a really rough day. My...my girlfriend was found murdered in Shively."

"Oh, I'm sorry," Jack replied, remorseful. "I imagine that is very painful for you. When they are girlfriends, they are special. It's when they become wives that things start to change."

Jack noticed Scott gave him a strange stare again. "Sorry," Jack said. "I went through a bitter divorce. I'm not too hip on wives and marriage. What brings you to the Judicial Center today?"

I'm looking for a red-haired man, who is a suspect in Chad Kennison's murder and maybe even in my girlfriend's, Scott knew, but did not share. *Could Chad have been with the Deputy Sheriff the night of his murder? Was he gay after all? Was Deputy Jack as well?* These outlandish questions flooded Scott's brain. "I...I need to go upstairs and check on something," Scott excused himself and started away toward the stairs.

"Nice seeing you again, detective," Jack decided to be polite. He found Scott to be a bit odd. But he could understand why he might be acting weird if his girlfriend had just been killed. Grief made people act strangely. Jack went back to watching the front door, his mundane routine.

His mind still unsettled, Scott climbed the stairs to the second floor. Instead of going to the Jury Pool Manager's office, he turned right and headed over to the Hall of Justice. Heading for the walkway back to Police Headquarters, he pondered, *Am I wasting my time looking for the man who was there that night? But what if Stacy is innocent?*

If the actual killer was a man, he would get away with murder and be free to kill again. And if this same person also murdered Debbie, he would get away with her murder as well. This troublesome uncertainty would not allow Scott to give up on his search for the red-haired man. He had to find out the identity of this person and what role he played in Chad's murder. He would focus his efforts on investigating Debbie's murder as well.

Scott went to the records room. He pulled the closed file on Renee Peterson's death. He took the file back to his desk. Roger was not at his desk. Scott was a bit relieved, because Roger would not appreciate him looking into the Renee Peterson case again.

Scott opened up Renee's file and rooted through the pictures. He pulled forth the close up pictures of the handcuffs. "They *are* his," he spoke aloud.

Surely, the fact that Jack has wavy, red hair is a coincidence. He could not have any part in Chad's or Debbie's murders. Could he? Jack's handcuffs seemed to be a direct match to the two pairs they found at Renee's suicide. And her death ruled as suicide had always bothered Scott. *What if Renee's death was* not *in fact a suicide? And what if Jack had something to do with her death? If he could be involved in something so atrocious, why couldn't he be involved in two stabbing deaths? And all three people were connected to the Judicial Center where Jack works: Renee, as an employee; Chad and Debbie, as members of the jury pool. Could it be possible Deputy Jack Jordan is our man?*

Scott did not want to believe this scenario, but a sick feeling plagued his stomach. If nothing else, he needed to investigate how two pairs of Deputy Jordan's handcuffs wound up at Renee's death site.

Chapter 20

Delight

He heard about Stacy Prescott's suspicion and questioning for Chad's and Debbie's murders. Thrilled by this delightful turn of events, it seemed he got away Scot-free with yet another gruesome murder. It grew more and more exciting with each one.

He had not meant to kill again so soon after Chad's murder, but he had not been able to resist the lure of doing in sweet, trusting Debbie. They ran into one another at the grocery store that weekend, and Debbie spoke to him. She remembered him from her time on jury duty.

When he arrived, uninvited, at her house, Monday evening, she ushered him in with a big, friendly smile, not suspicious at all about what he might be doing at her house. If they had been good friends, it would have been one thing, but they hardly knew one another.

She politely asked him if he would like something to drink. He followed her into the kitchen. Everything in the kitchen was in its place – no dirty dishes in the sink; the kitchen table clean and clear, with only a napkin holder and salt and pepper atop it; the stovetop glistened; the tile floor sparkled. *A perfect little housekeeper. The perfect woman,* he concluded, with loathing. He hated perfect people like her. They had it all. *I bet she even enjoys sex*, he pondered with disgust.

When she turned her back on him to get some glasses out of the cupboard, he pulled some gloves from his bag, slipped them on, pulled out a knife, and came up behind her. He put the sharp blade to her throat. *I'm going to mess up the floor in a second*, he thought with relish.

"Wha...what are you doing?" Debbie asked in alarm.

"I want you to back up very slowly, because I don't want to cut you." *Not yet. I want to watch you suffer first.*

He started to back up one step. Debbie felt the pressure of the knife at her throat, so she carefully moved backwards with him. *Just like Renee. So meek and agreeable.*

When they got to the middle of the floor, he removed the knife and asked Debbie to turn around. He wanted to see her face. He loved seeing the fear in their eyes. He missed this reaction with Chad, because it had been dark in the alley. But he heard him gasp and curse.

He reached in his bag and took out a pair of handcuffs. "Put these on one of your wrists. Put your hands behind your back, slip it on the other wrist, and snap them shut," he ordered.

"What do you want from me?" Debbie asked. "I don't have much, but you can take whatever you'd like. Just don't hurt me."

"Why would I hurt you, Debbie?" he asked. "If you do what I ask, you'll be fine. Now take the handcuffs and put them on as I asked you."

Debbie took the handcuffs. Her hands trembled as she slipped them on one wrist, placed her hands behind her back, slipped them on the other wrist, and snapped them shut.

"Good girl," He complimented with a smile. He pulled a chair away from the table and directed, "Now sit down in this chair. Your legs look a little shaky."

"They are," she confessed. "Why are you doing this?"

Renee had asked him this too. "Because I enjoy it," he honestly replied. "Do you enjoy being with your boyfriend?"

"What?" Debbie asked, looking perplexed.

"You know...sexually?"

This question rattled her. He could tell by her facial expression. *She's afraid to answer that question.* "We're just talking. I'm not going to go and tell him if you say no," he told her with a crazy laugh.

"Why do you want to know *that*?" she questioned.

"Because...you see...most women experience pleasure from sex. I get pleasure in another way. Do you know what that is?"

"No," she answered, her eyes huge and fixated on the knife. He held it straight up in front of him with both hands on the handle.

"It bothers you that I'm holding this knife, doesn't it?" he asked.

"Yes. Of course, it does," she admitted.

"Okay. I'll put it down," he offered with a wide smile.

He moved toward the table, as if he was going to sit the knife down there. When he saw a flash of relief in Debbie's eyes, his arm moved like lightening in the other direction. He swung the knife low and slashed her across her upper thighs and just above her pubic bone

"See what I mean? Better than sex!" he proclaimed.

One loud shriek escaped. He raised the knife again and ripped her entire throat open, severing her vocal cords. He pushed her head backwards to study his handwork. Blood gushed, and gurgling sounds slowly subsided.

Debbie's eyes and mouth remained wide open. Blood trickled down from the corners of her lips. He shoved her from her chair into the floor, fulfilling his personal vow that he would mess up the too 'perfect' floor.

He bent back down and sunk the knife between her legs, leaving it there. *Now Debbie knows what it feels like to be a freak.*

He pushed the chair back up to the table. *No sense leaving the kitchen a total wreck*, he thought with sick humor. He stepped over Debbie's body. He even hit the switch on the wall, turning the overhead kitchen light off. *No use wasting electricity. It's not like she needs the light to see anything*, he chuckled.

Before he stepped onto the plush, beige carpet in the hall, he took off his shoes and carried them. *In case there's blood on the bottom of my shoes.* He made his way down the hallway, looking for the bathroom. When he found it, he switched on the light in this room. He studied himself in the mirror, looking for blood on his clothes. He saw some on his arms and of course on his gloves. He pulled one of Debbie's pink towels off the rack by the sink. He wet down the end and carefully washed his arms. He even rinsed his gloves off a bit. He dried off with the other end of the towel. He wrapped his shoes in the towel, and he vacated the bathroom, turning off the light.

He walked through the living room and out the front door. A wide, satisfied smirk spread all across his face. His body quivered and tingled from head to toe. *I can get pleasure from physical relations – violent physical relations.* He skipped off to his car, happy to be alive, and to possess the capability to kill.

Chapter 21

Off the Hook

Wednesday morning, summoned back to Public Integrity, Scott discovered Roger and the medical examiner, Matt Smith, also there. "What's up?" he asked.

Howard Bugg, the head of the Public Integrity Unit, sat in his high back, black, leather chair behind his big wooden desk, his hands crossed and his thumbs tapping. A robust, daunting individual, his dark eyes almost appeared to be coal. When these eyes held a person in their sight, they pierced. Right now, these eyes penetrated through Scott.

Howard finally spoke. In his deep baritone voice, he told Scott, "What's up...is you were lucky this time. Matt tells me your girlfriend had been dead almost twenty-four hours when you found her. Roger claims you were on duty with him at the time of Debbie's murder. So you're being cleared as a suspect in Debbie's death."

"Good," Scott said, with a sigh. "I didn't want the investigation slowed by them looking at me."

"The department doesn't like to be put in a position where one of our people is looked at as a homicide suspect," Howard sternly reminded him, his eyes so harsh Scott looked away. "I know your actions were driven by your emotions, but in the future, you need to see that logic rules over emotion in this field. Have you got that?"

"Yes, sir," Scott answered, sheepishly looking him back in the eye.

"Good. I hope you do. I think you are going to make a great asset to the homicide squad. But another incident like this last one and someone may have to rethink your position."

"There won't be another incident like this one," Scott assured him.

"Good. Carry on," Howard said, talking to all of them now. He had other cases to investigate, and he knew these detectives and the medical examiner did as well.

Scott, Roger and Matt all filed out of Howard's office, shutting the door behind them. "So have you done an autopsy on Debbie yet?" Scott asked Matt as they walked down the bleak hallway. Fluorescent lights hung overhead, but the hallway still remained dark. The dark brown carpet and tan walls did nothing to brighten the area.

"Yes," Matt answered. As they meandered past several, other, closed, office doors, he explained, "Cause of death was the same as Chad Kennison. A fatal knife wound to the carotid. Her upper thighs and across her pubic bone were also slashed. And the murder weapon – an eight-inch chef's knife – was left in the genital area. This wound appeared to be almost postmortem. Her head appeared to have struck the ground, but this wound was also postmortem. The homicide squad deems she was sitting in a chair at the table with her hands cuffed behind her back when she was stabbed – both to the upper thighs and the fatal wound. I would guess the final wound, to the vaginal area, was done after she was lying in the floor. It was almost done as a kind of signature card."

"So if the killer is the same as Chad Kennison's, they are getting bolder as they go," Scott added his hypothesis. They all stopped to wait on an elevator.

"Which is not unusual for serial killers," Roger chimed in.

"I think the two murders have one and the same killer," Matt added his expert summation, as an elevator arrived and they all stepped aboard.

"Well, did the team find us any physical evidence to tie our prime suspect to Debbie's murder?" Roger asked.

"No. The killer did a bang up job of not leaving anything behind on this one. Forensics found no fingerprints on the knife. The homicide team found signs the killer cleaned up in the bathroom – minute traces of Debbie's blood. But they still uncovered no prints or DNA evidence. The killer was very thorough."

"Yeah. So it seems," Roger observed.

Roger and Scott parted ways with Matt then. They stepped off the elevator on the second floor. Matt's lab resided in another building, so he would ride the elevator down to the first floor.

"I don't think Stacy is smart enough to cover up everything like that," Scott commented to Roger, once they were on their own.

"Never underestimate a killer," Roger warned, as they entered their office area and walked toward their desks. "We still have motive for Stacy to have done this. A crime of passion. She thought Debbie was the woman in the alley with Chad, so she killed Chad first and then waited a while to go after Debbie. Debbie saw Stacy before, so she wasn't a stranger to her. This could explain why she opened her door to her. There was no sign of breaking and entering, so it looks as if Debbie knew her killer."

"That's just it. Debbie opening the door to Stacy does *not* make sense. Debbie was freaked out when I told her Stacy was our prime suspect in Chad's murder. And Stacy threatened her at the Judicial Center. Why would she open the door to her? Debbie wasn't stupid."

"You have a point. But I think the Commonwealth Attorney will try and tie the two murders together. The MO is the same, and like I said, Stacy had motive."

"So we are not going to keep pursuing this case?"

"If something else comes to light that points to another suspect, yes," Roger told him, taking a seat at his desk. "But with what we have to go on now, Stacy is our one, and only, suspect. And we have nothing to go on to point us in another direction."

Except for handcuffs from another possible *murder and a red-haired deputy, who Debbie would have trusted*, Scott thought, but kept to himself, as he also sat down at his own desk. He did not intend to let his suspicions go unearthed. He had to have some answers to the questions still lingering in his mind.

Chapter 22

He Said; She Said

Scott waited about an hour. He worked on some paperwork at his desk, even though his mind was not on it. Then he excused himself to Roger and went over to the Judicial Center to talk with Deputy Jordan again.

Deputy Jordan once again watched the front entrance. "Jack, can you take a break for a few moments?" Scott asked him, as he came through the metal detectors.

As usual, two other deputy sheriffs presided there as well. Jack addressed them both and asked if they could handle the door alone for a few minutes. They both smiled and assured him they could. The majority of the time, they stood around and talked to one another. They did not need three people watching the door, but it was protocol to go overboard on security since 9-11.

Jack stepped off to the side a little. "What did you need, detective?" he asked.

"I wanted to ask you a few questions," Scott told him.

"About what?" Jack asked. "You guys aren't still investigating Renee's death, are you? I thought that was ruled a suicide."

Scott studied Jack's eyes for a moment, trying to determine if Jack looked worried. He looked more intrigued than anything.

"Actually, we did rule her death as a suicide. But my question does deal with her death...in a way."

"Okay," Jack replied. He looked relaxed and agreeable. "What do you need to know?"

"Um...I noticed your handcuffs yesterday."

"My handcuffs," Jack repeated, reaching to finger them. "What have they got to do with Renee?"

Scott reached into a pocket on the inside of his suit jacket. He pulled forth a photo he took from Renee's file. "Renee handcuffed her ankles to the railroad track. This is a picture of the handcuffs. They are engraved...just like yours...with JCJ. Are they your handcuffs?"

Jack took the photo from Scott and took a good, hard look at it. Startled, he answered, "They...yes, they are mine." He seemed a little shaken as he handed the photo back.

"Any idea how Renee ended up with two sets of your handcuffs?" Scott inquired.

"None," Jack answered with assurance. He moved even farther away from the door now, suddenly concerned about this conversation being overheard.

"Had you lost any handcuffs around the time of Renee's death?" Scott continued to question.

"No...not exactly," Jack answered, looking down at his shoes and toeing the ground with one.

"Care to explain that," Scott prodded. *He looks a little nervous now.*

"I gave two pairs to an ex-girlfriend," Jack confessed almost in a whisper. He made sweeping eye contact with Scott before he studied the floor again. "She was...you know... into the kinky stuff."

"So did Renee have contact with this ex-girlfriend?" Scott asked.

"Every single day," Jack replied, looking Scott in the eye again. "It was Jeanette O'Riley. Assistant Jury Manager, Jeanette O'Riley, one of Renee's co-workers. The woman who is now conveniently married to Renee's widower, Mitchell. In fact, the two of them married before Renee was hardly cold. Are you thinking Renee's death was murder instead of suicide?" he now questioned.

The plot thickens, Scott was contemplating. He had not anticipated this unexpected turn of events. *Jeanette has short, curly red hair as well. Could she have killed Renee because she wanted her husband? Stacy said Chad was with a woman who looked a lot like her. Jeanette does. But what motive would she have had to kill Chad? And Debbie?*

"Detective," Jack called, troubled by his odd silence.

"Sorry," Scott apologized. "I appreciate you talking with me, Jack."

"No problem. But you didn't answer my question. Are you thinking Renee's death was murder instead of suicide? Jeanette is a cold bitch. She moved right in on Renee's widower, and she's adopted Renee's daughter. If you are looking at this as a homicide, then you need to look closely at Jeanette."

"Thanks, Jack," Scott said again. "We aren't necessarily reopening this case. I just wanted to clear up the confusion about the handcuffs, and now you've done that for me."

"But why would Jeanette give the handcuffs to Renee? What if she used them on her instead, and Renee's death wasn't a suicide?"

"We don't know this," Scott argued. Jack had raised his voice, and strangers walking by looked at them. "I need to run upstairs. But I appreciate you taking the time to talk with me."

"Go. Run upstairs. Go to Jeanette's office and question her," Jack almost ordered.

Where Scott was going and what he intended to do, he did not share with Jack. He did not want Jack following him. The element of surprise in questioning Jeanette was much too important to Scott.

His heart raced as he took the steps two at a time. *What if we have the wrong person in custody? What if Stacy had nothing to do with Chad and Debbie's murders? What if Jeanette is a serial killer and has killed three people?* His mind all at once flooded with questions and conjectures, he had to have crucial answers right away.

* * * *

Jeanette and Charly sat at their desk in the office. Charly saw him first, so she approached the counter to help him. "Hi, detective. What can we do for you today?" She asked, being friendly and polite. Every time she saw Scott it brought back terrible memories of Renee. So he was not one of her favorite people.

"I actually need to speak with Jeanette," he told Charly, pointing in Jeanette's direction.

She looked up at the sound of her name, surprised to hear the detective asking for her. She got up from her desk at once and approached the front counter, standing beside Charly. "What do you need to see me about, detective?" she asked.

Scott's eyes took in her appealing cleavage. Jeanette's low, V-neck blouse, with the top two buttons undone, showcased this attribute. *The other hair and saliva found at the murder scene tested male. Could Jeanette have had a sex change? She certainly is all female.*

Scott forced his eyes to look away from her bust line. He studied her hair instead – red, short and curly. "Um...is there someplace we could talk in private?" he asked, making eye contact with Jeanette for the first time.

"I need to go and call some potential jurors," Charly chirped. "Amy, our assistant, is on break for about fifteen minutes. So you can have the office all to yourselves."

"Thanks," Scott said and gave her a slight smile.

"Sure," Charly said. She disappeared behind the wall then. She did not come out into the lobby in front of the counter. Instead, she opened a security door that led directly into the hallway.

Scott heard the door unlatch and then he heard it shut. He turned a bit and looked through the glass doors leading into the office space. He watched Charly heading away toward the assembly room down the hall.

"Would you like to come back here and sit in my office?" Jeanette offered.

"No. That's not necessary," Scott said. He did not want her to get comfortable. Standing at the counter was a good place to talk.

"So what do we need to talk about?" she asked, eyeballing him strangely.

"What I need to ask you is somewhat of a delicate issue," Scott began.

"Delicate?" she questioned, looking puzzled.

"Yeah. You see, I've discovered the handcuffs Renee had around her ankles the night she died belonged to a deputy sheriff who works here at the Judicial Center."

"Renee had handcuffs around her ankles?" Jeanette asked. She looked distressed by the news.

Is this news really shocking and upsetting to her, or is she playing up her emotions to make it look that way? Scott pondered. "Yes. She handcuffed herself to the tracks."

"Oh, God! She *was* crazy, wasn't she?" Jeanette declared, shaking her head. "Mitch and I have talked a lot about Renee since...since her suicide. We're just relieved she didn't hurt Susanna, like some mothers do that have postpartum depression."

"You're married to Renee's widower, right?" Scott inquired.

"Yes. We married shortly after Renee's death. I've taken a lot of grief about that – from everyone imaginable. But Renee's illness ended her marriage way before her death did. Mitch and Susanna deserved to be happy."

"Did you know Renee's marriage was in trouble before her death?" Scott asked.

"No. I only knew Renee was depressed."

"She never talked to you about her marriage?" he pressed, reaching to scratch his chin.

"Not really. She talked more about herself. Depressed people tend to be wrapped up in themselves," Jeanette explained.

She keeps stressing that Renee was depressed, Scott observed. "Well...back to the handcuffs. I tracked down the deputy sheriff the handcuffs belonged to. I thought maybe he gave them to Renee. But he tells me he gave them to you instead."

"To me?" Jeanette questioned, placing her hands on her hips. "Why would a deputy sheriff give me his handcuffs?" she asked, feigning ignorance.

"Uh...he claims the two of you were having an affair. And that you...well..." He tapped a knuckle to his bottom lips before he revealed, "You were into some 'kinky' stuff."

"Would this deputy sheriff happen to be Jack Jordan?" Jeanette asked. Her eyes narrowed and looked angry.

"Why do you ask? Were you having an affair with Deputy Jordan?" Scott answered her question with a few more questions.

"He'd like to think so," Jeanette accused. "My husband wanted to swear out an E.P.O. against Jack Jordan. Now...I'm thinking...maybe we should have. That man is crazy as hell!" Jeanette proclaimed.

"Why would your husband want to swear out an E.P.O. against Deputy Jordan?" Scott inquired, rocking back on his heel.

"Because he threatened us both. He confronted me twice in the cafeteria...once when Mitch and I started dating, and another time after we got married. He called me a heartless bitch and a loser, and he said we would both be sorry one day and get what was coming to us. Mitch came here and told Jack to leave me alone. Jack said I was a cold bitch and Mitch was a heartless bastard. He also told him he better watch his back. Like I said, he threatened us both."

"Why would Deputy Jordan act in such a manner?" Scott questioned, fingering his chin again. He was not sure who to believe now. *Jack had been in a hurry for him to come upstairs and question Jeanette. And he wanted to pass the blame off on her about the handcuffs. Maybe he lied to save his own butt.*

"Who knows," she replied, crossing her arms across her chest. "He went through a nasty divorce from his wife of many years. She got everything – house and nice car. Jack's been weird ever since. Ask Charly. She'll back me up. He went off on her about having to work security for a rock star one day. Basically said they were all drugged out degenerates who deserved to die. He's whacked I tell you. You don't think he had something to do with Renee's death, do you? Could it have been murder instead of suicide? My God!"

"No. I'm not accusing anyone of anything like that," Scott assured her. "I was just tying up some loose ends." *If Deputy Jordan was mad at the world, and he killed Renee, maybe he found a reason to kill Chad. Maybe the fact he was a rich playboy disgusted him. But what reason would he have had to kill Debbie?*

"The handcuffs were not mine. I never had an affair with Jack. Except for in his dreams," Jeanette staunchly maintained. She uncrossed her arms and placed her hands against the counter instead. "I need to go call my husband and tell him what lies Jack is spreading. You are welcome to talk to my husband about how Jack threatened him as well."

"Jeanette, I didn't mean to upset you," Scott consoled, reaching to pat her hand. *Her hand feels soft like a woman's. Obviously, Jack is a* male. *So it's more plausible his DNA would match to the other hair from Chad Kennison's murder. Jack was my initial suspect. Could this deputy sheriff be crazy and killing people?*

No closer to an answer than when he had first come over to the Judicial Center, if anything, Scott was even more befuddled. *Someone is lying, and I need to determine who this person is.*

"Are we through here, detective?" Jeanette asked, pulling back from the counter.

Scott could tell she was eager to get to her desk. *She's going to call her husband. This thing could get very ugly now.* He may have opened an enormous can of worms. He needed to go talk to Deputy Jordan again.

"Yes. Thanks for your cooperation, Jeanette," he said.

"Sure," she rather absently responded. She turned and rushed away toward her cubicle.

Scott rotated and left the office. He raced back down the stairs. He walked up behind Jack and tapped him on the shoulder.

As soon as Jack turned, he asked, "Did you talk to Jeanette? What did she have to say?"

"She claims the two of you never had an affair. She says you never gave her any handcuffs. She also said you threatened her on two occasions and her husband on one."

"Lying bitch!" he exclaimed, placing his hands on his rounded belly. The other two deputies turned to look his way. He waved off their concern. Strangers coming into the building also gave a curious glance again as they walked past.

"Did you threaten Jeanette and her husband?" Scott asked, staying on task. Jack's body stiffened and his fists curled. *He seems to detest Jeanette.*

"All I did was call a spade a spade. Jeanette's actions disgusted me. So I told her exactly what I thought of her...in not so nice terms. As to her husband, he got in *my* face. We were standing almost where you and I are now. There were other deputies present that can testify to the confrontation. In fact, one almost stepped in because they thought he was going to get physical with me."

"Did you tell him to watch his back," Scott questioned, tapping his index fingers.

"Yeah. But I didn't mean from me. I meant from the lying, cheating slut he married. I bet she is whoring around on him."

"You hate Jeanette, don't you, Jack?" Scott prodded, tapping those same fingers on his chin.

"Yes, I do. I'll admit that," Jack professed, spewing steam. "Now more than ever. She and that husband of hers deserve to burn in hell!"

Jack's face turned beet red; his icy blue eyes protruded; his teeth gnashed. He looked mentally ill. *But is he?* "Jack, would you mind giving me a fingerprint and DNA sample?"

"I can't believe you are asking a fellow officer of the law to do this," Jack commented, his anger turning to incredulousness.

"Is that a yes or a no?" Scott pushed, dropping his hands to his waist.

"This just shows what this world is coming to. It used to be that fellow officers stuck up for fellow officers. But no more. You believe that crazy bitch's lies over my words?"

"I don't know what to believe right now, Jack," Scott answered. "You could help me clear up the confession by cooperating with giving a fingerprint and DNA sample."

"You know what, you snot-nosed fool, I have nothing to hide. But I'm an officer of the law, so I know my rights. If you want a DNA and fingerprint sample from me, then get a warrant. While you are at it, Sparky, why don't you get one to obtain Jeanette's as well? Then you might discover who is lying."

"So you are refusing to voluntarily give me a fingerprint and DNA sample?" Scott verified.

"Yes. And I am done talking to you!" Jack snapped. "You disgust me! You are an abomination to the LMPD police force!" he added, spraying slight spittle in Scott's face.

Scott backed away. *I'm done here*, he knew. He needed to see if he could get a warrant to collect DNA and fingerprint samples. And he *did* intend to see if he could get one for *both* Deputy Jack Jordan and Mrs. Jeanette Peterson. One of them was lying, and this crucial bit of evidence could possibly tell Scott which one was not telling the truth. If one of these people's DNA matched to the hair found at Chad Kennison's murder, it could also tie that individual to a murder scene. *I have probable cause to follow up on this important lead,* Scott was convinced. He raced out the exit door and began jogging toward his building.

Chapter 23

Heard It Through the Grapevine

Scott practically turned his chair over at his desk as he bounced into it. "What have you been?" Roger questioned.

"I've been following up on some leads," Scott told him. "I need to get some warrants to obtain fingerprints and DNA from two people."

"For what case?" Roger asked, giving Scott his full attention now. He even turned his chair in his direction.

"The Renee Peterson, Chad Kennison, and Debbie Gray cases. I believe they are all tied together," he revealed. He rocked in his chair with nervous energy.

"What does Renee Peterson's suicide have to do with anything? How could it be tied to two homicides?" he probed. His brow puckered, and his mouth grew tight.

"Look at this picture of the handcuffs Renee had around her ankles," Scott directed, taking the photo from his suit jacket again. He handed it across the desk to Roger.

Roger begrudgingly took the picture from Scott's outstretched hand. Glancing at it, he said, "Yeah. So?"

"As I pointed out when we were still investigating her death, the handcuffs are engraved."

"Okay. Can you please get to the point?" Roger prodded, sounding impatient.

"My point is I saw a matching pair of these handcuffs on a deputy sheriff at the Judicial Center yesterday."

"So you are saying these handcuffs belonged to a deputy sheriff at the Judicial Center. I'm still not following what this fact has to do with our homicides."

"The handcuffs belong to Deputy Jackson Charles Jordan. He has wavy, red hair. He also had ready access to all three victims. All three victims would have trusted him. Debbie's house wasn't broken into that I could see, so she must have let the murderer in. It had to have been someone she knew and/or trusted. Did you guys find any sign of forced entry?"

"No," Roger answered, handing the picture back to Scott. "But Renee Peterson's death was deemed a suicide. We still have no evidence to prove otherwise. The fact that she had two pairs of Deputy Jordan's handcuffs does not make him a murderer. Of her or anyone else."

"We have some male, red hair, found at the Chad Kennison murder site. There was a man there too. There were handcuffs used in Renee, Chad's and Debbie's murders," he said, pointing to the handcuffs on Renee's ankles again.

"The handcuffs used in Chad's and Debbie's murders weren't engraved. There is no way to tie them back to Jack Jordan. All you have is supposition here, Scott. For all we know, Jack may have given Renee a few pairs of his handcuffs for some reason. Or maybe she somehow stole them."

"No. He claims he gave them to the Assistant Jury Manager, Jeanette. He claimed Jeanette and he were having an affair; she was a bit into the kinky stuff, so that's why he gave her the two sets of handcuffs. She claims the affairs never happened. One of them is lying. If I could just get warrants to collect their fingerprints and DNA, I could find out if either of them have any ties to Renee's murder and/or Chad's."

"So who are you looking at...the deputy...or Jeanette?" Roger could not help but question, crossing his arms and shaking his head. He grew wearier of this conversation by the minute.

"I'm not sure," Scott honestly answered, laying the picture on his desk. "But I questioned Deputy Jordan, Roger. He's a very bitter man. He's threatened the Assistant Jury Manager on two occasions and her husband on another. He seems to be a little off the deep end. As to Jeanette, she is now married to Renee's widower. She married him shortly after Renee's death. So she may have had motive for getting Renee out of the way. She also has short, red, curly hair, by the way. But unless her DNA tests male, which I have serious doubts of, then I would lean toward Jack being our man."

"There's only one problem with this theory," Roger said, leaning back in his chair. "The only thing that even remotely ties him to Chad's murder is his red hair. But he isn't the only red-haired male in Louisville. And Stacy led us to believe Chad was with a woman. Do you think Deputy Jordan dresses in drag too?"

"But Stacy could be lying about this," Scott pointed out, shaking his index finger in Roger's direction. "She wants us to think the bloody clothes belonged to the killer. So he would have had to have been dressed as a woman. But if she is lying, Chad could have been with a man. Maybe he swung both ways. He seemed to be highly sexually motivated."

"Darrell is seeking an indictment of Stacy Prescott for Chad's murder," Roger reminded him, sitting up straight in his chair. "She had motive for murder. Her DNA links her to the scene and the DNA from the hairs found on the bloody clothing matches to her. We also have her fingerprint on Chad's body. We have a pretty airtight case against her. We are looking for evidence to tie her to Debbie's murder, since the MO was the same. We already know they had a heated confrontation. Maybe the man with Chad *was* promenading as a woman. And perhaps Stacy thought this woman was Debbie. That would give her motive to kill her too. Two crimes of passion. Makes much more sense than Deputy Jordan going on a killing rampage. And we have evidence to back us up in Stacy's involvement – at least with Chad's homicide. Renee's suicide is old news. You need to put that case to bed, and put it to bed once and for all," Roger coached. "As to finding the redheaded man who was involved with Chad, let's not waste our time. The evidence does *not* warrant us doing so. Let's focus on either tying Debbie's murder in with Chad's or finding another killer. The only thing we can prove the red-haired man with Chad was guilty of was being gay and of some illicit sexual folly. Let this aspect of the case go, rookie. We have a solid case against Stacy Prescott. Darrell is going after her with both barrels."

Roger's phone rang then. He rolled his chair back behind his desk and snatched it up. "We'll be right over," he said with urgency, lowering the phone. "You've stirred up a shit load of trouble," he said to Scott.

"What? How so?" he asked.

"Mitchell Peterson just took a slug at Deputy Jordan over at the Judicial Center. He was ranting and raving about how you said Jack had something to do with his first wife's death and how Jack was spreading lies about his second. We need to get over there and try to straighten this mess out as best we can."

"I knew it was going to get ugly," Scott commented under his breath as he and Roger rushed toward the doors.

Over at the Judicial Center within minutes, they found that the deputy sheriffs had Mitchell handcuffed and subdued. He sat in a chair by the window. Holding an icepack to one eye, Deputy Jack talked to Lieutenant Colonel Edward Samuels, head of the Major Crimes Division. A short and stocky man, with white cotton hair, only in his forties, he looked much older.

Through his one good eye, as Jack spied Scott approaching, he pushed past the lieutenant colonel. "What's that bastard doing here again?" he demanded to know, advancing toward Scott and pointing a jabbing finger toward him.

"I'll handle this, Jack," Edward assured him. "You need to simmer down."

"That's easy for you to say, Ed. You weren't the one falsely accused of a homicide and slugged by some mad man."

"I know, Jack. I'm sorry," Edward apologized. "Let me handle this. He's one of my men. He will not bother you any further," he pledged.

"Fine," Jack growled, turning and walking a few paces away. He turned to watch though.

The lieutenant colonel approached Scott and Roger. "Detective Arnold," he bellowed in a no-nonsense tone of voice.

"Yes, sir," Scott replied. This conversation was not going to be a good one.

Edward grabbed him by the arm and led him off to the side of the x-ray machine and metal detectors. "What the hell were you thinking, son?! Why were you questioning a long-term, commendable, deputy sheriff about a closed case? You've stirred up a hornet's nest."

"I'm sorry about that," Scott apologized, but clearly showed no real remorse. "Two matching, engraved handcuffs were found at the scene of Renee Peterson's death. And...I have reason to believe her murder might tie into Chad Kennison's and...and my girlfriend Debbie's murders."

Edward had heard about Detective Arnold's girlfriend's homicide. He had sympathy for Scott, but he could not let him overstep his boundaries due to grief. "I think your grief is making you do crazy things!" Edward accused. "Let's get one thing straight here. We are all on the same team. The Commonwealth Attorney is presenting to the Grand Jury next week for two indictments against Stacy Prescott – one for Chad's murder and another for your girlfriend's. I don't need you working for the defense by digging up non-essential facts they can use against Darrell. You need to cease and desist with your current investigation. Have you got that?"

"Yes, sir," Scott answered. "I just want to make sure we have the right person."

"We do," Edward assured him. "We have tons of evidence to prove it. You need to stay away from the deputy sheriff and stop working on closed cases. All you need to be concerned with now is testifying in court against Stacy Prescott. Do we understand one another?"

"Yes. We do," Scott agreed.

"Good. Roger, rein this wildcard in. Okay?"

"I'll do my best," Roger promised.

Edward turned and walked away then, going to apologize to Deputy Jordan one more time. He also attempted to convince Jack *not* to file charges of assault against Mitchell Peterson. He wanted this whole incident to be put to bed, without jail time for anyone. However, Jack had every right to press charges, and if he refused to back down, then Edward would have to take Mitchell Peterson into custody.

Roger watched Lieutenant Colonel Samuels talking with Jack. He turned his attention back on Scott. Grabbing him by the shoulder, Roger stressed, "I don't want to hear anymore about Renee Peterson or who the male red hair at the Chad Kennison murder belonged to. These are dead issues now. Have you got that?"

"Got it loud and clear," Scott said with aversion. "I need to take a little walk and clear my head."

"Take a walk," Roger agreed. "Your dealings with Deputy Jordan and the Assistant Jury Manager are through," he stressed one final time.

Scott charged off, sulking. He had become a detective at a young age because of his tenaciousness in investigations. Now, ordered to ignore something that might be a piece of crucial evidence, anger and frustration filled him. But since no one seemed to be behind him, he knew he must do what was being asked of him.

He barreled out the exit doors, almost plowing down two other men. Out on the city street, he paused to look at the Judicial Center one last time. He shook his head with discontentment, turned and marched off in the other direction. He would walk around the city until he cooled off and made himself accept the decisions of his superiors. It was going to be a *very* long walk.

Chapter 24

The Arrest

The following week, on Friday, the Grand Jury handed down an indictment against Stacy Prescott for the homicide of Chad Kennison. There was not enough evidence for them to grant an indictment for Debbie Gray's murder. Darrell did not care. He still intended to try and tie the two murders together at trial.

Roger and Scott showed up at her house Friday afternoon about 2:00 p.m. with an arrest warrant. The housekeeper, a petite Mexican woman, answered the door.

Roger told her, "I'm Detective Matthews. This is Detective Arnold. We need to speak with Stacy, please."

"She's in her room studying for exams at school," the maid told them.

"Well, can you call her to the door for us, please?" Roger requested.

The housekeeper looked a little wary to do so, but because they were officers of the law, she nodded. "Come in," she told them.

She led them into the foyer. Scott shut the door behind him. The maid walked away and left them standing there.

Several minutes passed. Scott glanced at the Prescott family photographs along the entranceway walls. As usual, in pictures, they looked like the perfect, happy family – no worries in the world. This scenario was about to change.

Stacy came down the foyer toward them. She had a frightened look in her eyes. "I called my attorney," she told them.

"That's good," Roger said. With a grave expression, he pulled forth the arrest warrant. "Stacy Prescott, you are under arrest for the murder of Chad Kennison," he announced.

Stacy looked as if she stuck her finger in an electric socket – her body shuddered; her mouth dropped open; her eyes enlarged into giant circles. Before Roger could continue with her Miranda rights, she let out a loud shriek, proclaiming, "No! This can't be happening! No!"

Stacy grew hysterical then. She dropped to her knees in front of them and half pleaded, "You...you...ca...can't a...arrest me!" She began to wail, and her body shook like jelly.

Scott looked unsure as to what to do. He still had a bad feeling about arresting Stacy. But he ceased looking into Deputy Jordan and Jeanette's possible connection with Chad's murder. He still wished he could tie up all the loose ends. But he realized he could not. He could not help but feel sorry for Stacy though. *She looks so young and innocent. Could she really have committed two such atrocious homicides?*

When the housekeeper came over to comfort her, bending and placing her hands on her shoulders, Stacy demanded, "Juanita, c...call da...daddy!"

The maid left her side at once and went to call Donald Prescott. Roger ignored Stacy's tirade and continued with her Miranda rights. "Stacy, you have the right to remain silent. If you give up that right, anything you say can, and will, be used against you in a court of law."

Stacy continued to blubber, not listening to a single word Roger uttered. He continued to recite her rights anyway. When he finished, he bent to grasp one of her arms. "You need to come with us," he told Stacy in a gruff voice.

"I…I want to…to wait…to wait for…my…daddy," she stuttered in a whiny voice, sounding even more like a child.

"He can come to Metro Corrections to see you. I have a warrant for your arrest. There is nothing he can do to stop this from happening. Neither can your attorney. You need to get up, Stacy."

Scott looked away as her pleading eyes locked with his. *The evidence points to her as the killer. Even if she does look like nothing but a frightened child*, he tried to convince himself.

Scott forced his feet to move. He went over on the other side of Stacy and took her other arm. Together, Roger and he forced Stacy to rise. They walked her partially limp body out of the house and to an awaiting LMPD squad car.

A police officer took charge of her then. He placed her in handcuffs and folded her into the back of his patrol car. Stacy lay over in the seat, still crying.

"Geez, this one is a real basket case," the young officer commented to both Roger and Scott, before he climbed into the front seat of his police car. He would take her to Metro Corrections and they would book her.

If she's hysterical now, it's only the beginning of a bad evening for her, Scott pondered as he watched the police car back out of the driveway.

"Our role in this case is over, rookie. That is, other than to testify in court," Roger told him with a satisfied smirk.

Scott walked away by his side, sickened.

* * * *

At Louisville Metro Corrections Department, Stacy was turned over to a tough looking, female, corrections officer. A little on the heavy side, she looked solid rather than flabby. Her sandy brown hair was pulled back in a tight ponytail and her hazel eyes bulged. This officer ordered her to strip in front of her. Stacy stared at her in disbelief.

"What's the matter with you? Are you deaf? Get those clothes off. Now!" she barked in an even more stern voice. Her voice almost sounded masculine. She also held her body more like a man.

Stacy slowly undressed in front of this woman, sheepishly glancing at her from time to time. The woman gave her a hard, icy stare the whole time. Stacy shivered, not from the cold but from emotional trauma. A sea of tears escaped, rolling down her pale cheeks and dripping off her chin.

When she undressed, the correctional officer shocked and appalled Stacy even more. She put on plastic gloves and roughly performed a body cavity search. She reached inside private, female areas and callously pushed and probed. Stacy stifled a gag. She could not believe this woman performed this exploration on her. She felt sexually assaulted.

When the officer finished her search, finding nothing, she peeled off her gloves and threw them in a nearby trash container. Then she picked up an orange, cotton pantsuit, with METRO CORRECTIONS written in big bold lettering on the back. She shoved this garment into Stacy's arms. "Put this on!" she ordered.

Stacy quickly covered her naked, ravaged body with the garments, thankful to be able to shield her private parts once more. The woman took a death grip on Stacy's arm then. She led her away to be photographed and fingerprinted.

After they took mug-shots of Stacy from several angles and fingerprinted her, she was led away to the women's dormitory. Horrified to discover several other women in this barred area, as she was placed in the cell, Stacy's body quivered. She tried not to look at these other women – these mean looking strangers. She turned and faced the bars. She jumped when the corrections officer slid the jail cell door closed with a bang.

"What, have we gots a little miss ainti-social here?" One of the black ladies spoke.

Stacy ignored her. She reached out to grip the jail bars. She wanted to scream, but she knew it would do no good.

"Hey, bitch, I'm talkin' to you," the woman spoke again. She walked over and clutched Stacy's upper arm.

"Leave her alone," a Hispanic woman chipped in, coming to Stacy's defense. "She ain't botherin' nobody."

"Who the hell ya think you is, my mama?" the black woman asked, releasing Stacy and turning to the Hispanic woman instead.

Stacy glanced behind her with fear in her eyes. She watched as the two women posted up. *I've got to get out of here!* She contemplated with terror.

As if her thoughts had been heard, a guard approached the cell once more. The black woman and the Hispanic parted.

"Stacy Prescott," he called.

"Th…that's me," she stammered. *Am I about to be released?* She half prayed. Her hope of this miracle coming true escalated as she saw the guard take out his keys.

"Yeah. Get the little white-class bitch out of here," the loudmouthed, black woman proclaimed, as Stacy was led from the cell.

The guard ignored this woman. He placed handcuffs on Stacy, and he led her away. "Where am I going?" she asked, very expectant this man would tell her she was going home.

"Your lawyer is here and wants to have a chat with you," he told her in a very matter-of-fact voice. He continued to lead her down the hall toward a conference room.

When he opened the door and Stacy saw Stuart McClain standing there, she dashed into his arms. He awkwardly gave her a hug. She burst into tears once more. Stuart hated that she was crying, although not because he cared. He did not want his suit messed up with her mucus and makeup.

He eased Stacy back from him as soon as he could. "Here, sit down," he told her, pulling out a chair.

Stacy's legs wobbled, so she did as asked. "Can you get me out of here, Stuart," she begged.

He sat down on the other side of the table. "Not yet," he gingerly broke the news to her. "You have to go through arraignment first. And that will be tomorrow morning…"

"To…tomorrow morning! I can't stay here overnight!" Stacy protested. She looked terrified.

"Stacy…it will be alright," he tried to pacify her.

"No…no it won't!" she argued. "Some officer stuck her fingers in my…in…in places she shouldn't have. Then some black woman in the cell with me called me a bitch and grabbed me by the arm. Some Hispanic woman tried to help, and the two of them were about to fight. That's when the guard got me out. I'll be killed if I stay here, Stuart. I don't belong here. You've got to do something," she beseeched him with panic.

"I'll get you moved to a private cell," he promised, not certain if he could pull this maneuver off or not. He would flash some money around and see what he could do.

"You promise?" Stacy verified.

"I promise," he lied. *Money usually moves mountains.* "Right now, Stacy, we need to talk about the arraignment tomorrow." He led her back on subject. "That's when we'll get you out of this place."

That's all Stacy wanted – to get out of this hellish place. "Okay," she agreed, calming down a little. She still did not want to spend the night in this Godforsaken place, but if she could at least be moved to a private cell, she thought she could endure it. She tried to focus on what Stuart said about the arraignment – her ticket out of this nightmare.

* * * *

The next morning, led into the courtroom by Deputy Jordan, Stacy looked shell-shocked. Stuart moved her to a private cell, but women in other nearby cells still taunted and called her names all night long. Stacy had been unable to sleep, for fear one of these other inmates would somehow get into her cell and do her harm. She kept her eyes wide open and her ears tuned all night long.

Now, Stacy sat at a small table, beside Stuart McClain, and she stared into space. Her father sat right behind her. A low wall separated his seated place from Stacy and Stuart's. The Commonwealth Attorney and a female assistant sat across the aisle from them at another small table. Both attorneys dressed impeccably, in expensive suits, shirts with cufflinks, and ties.

They all rose to their feet, to give proper respect, as the judge, Aretha Washington, entered the chambers. Her black robe flowed as she climbed two small steps and ascended to the bench. Aretha, a large, African American woman, often found on the side of the defendant.

When the judge was seated, the Commonwealth Attorney and his assistant both sat down. Stuart and Stacy remained standing. Aretha read the charges against Stacy, "Stacy Prescott, you are charged with the homicide of Chad Kennison. How do you plead?"

"N…not guilty, Your Honor," she answered in a small, shaky voice. *Not guilty* – the statement Stuart told her to make.

"Very well. This case will be scheduled for trial. We will proceed with the bail hearing," she announced, folding her hands.

Stacy took a weary seat as the Commonwealth Attorney stood. Stuart McClain remained standing. In a deep, authoritative voice, Stuart beckoned the judge's attention first. He stared her right in the eye and announced himself, "Your Honor, Stuart McClain, representing the defendant."

"Your Honor, Darrell Adams representing the Commonwealth," Darrell also announced himself, making constant eye contact as well.

Stuart wasted no time addressing the judge again. "Your Honor, if it pleases the court, I ask that my client, Stacy Prescott, be granted bail immediately."

"Your Honor," Darrell also addressed her. "With all due respect, his client, Stacy Prescott, has been accused of a heinous crime. And LMPD detectives are in the process of gathering evidence to tie her to a second homicide, which would make her a serial killer. She is a threat to society. She should be denied bail."

"Your Honor, this is totally ridiculous!" Stuart argued, rolling his eyes at Darrell. "My client comes from a very upstanding family in the community. If granted bail, she will be released to the recognizance of her father, Donald Prescott." He pointed behind him then at Donald. The judge's eyes followed his finger. She had been looking back and forth between the two attorneys as they addressed her and argued their cases.

Seeing the judge's perusal of his client's father, Stuart continued, "Stacy Prescott poses no flight hazard. And she is innocent until proven guilty of the 'heinous crime' that the

Commonwealth Attorney alluded to. And they have no evidence whatsoever tying her to a second homicide."

"Your Honor," Darrell called, garnering her attention and eye contact once more. "We have plenty of DNA and circumstantial evidence directly tying Stacy Prescott to one, grisly homicide. She is a danger to society. She should be held in custody until her trial," he fought back.

"Preposterous!" Stuart disputed again. "Innocent until proven guilty, Your Honor," he stressed again. He glanced at Darrell once more and shook his head, as if to say, *Don't you even know the law?*

"Probable cause, Your Honor," Darrell rebutted. "We have a very strong case against Stacy Prescott."

"Okay…enough, gentlemen," she silenced them both with a dismissive wave of her hand. "I could listen to you argue all day, and we would get nowhere. I read the pretrial report on the charges against Ms. Prescott. I also received a memorandum and certain supporting documents from the defendant's attorney, Mr. McClain. I have had an opportunity to read not only the Pretrial Services report, but also the materials filed by Mr. McClain. These documents attest to the fact that the defendant is from a very respectable family and has no prior offenses. Is there anything else that's been filed on this issue by any party to this case?"

"No, Your Honor," Both attorneys answered.

"Okay. Stacy Prescott, will you please stand?" she requested.

Stacy did as was asked of her. As she looked into the imposing face of the judge once more, she trembled and tears came to her eyes. "Stacy Prescott, I'm releasing you into the recognizance of your father," she heard the judge announce.

Stacy twirled and threw her shuddering body into the arms of her father. She did not even hear the rest of what the judge said. Both grateful for her release, the fact that the judge imposed a one million dollar bail did not faze either Stacy or her father.

The judge further instructed, "Mr. Prescott, please see our bail bondsman to make arrangements for your daughter's release." Then she said in conclusion, "Good day, everyone."

"Well, we gave it our best shot," Darrell said, with disappointment, to his assistant. As he vacated his spot, he walked over to Stuart McClain. "I'll see you in court, Stuart," he half threatened.

"It will be a pleasure," Stuart smugly replied. Darrell headed toward the door and his assistant followed.

Stacy Prescott was a free woman again – *at least for now*.

Chapter 25

Disposable

Mitch's tie squeezed around his neck, suspending his airflow. But he tolerated this discomfort. He could not stop now. Nearing the point of ecstasy, he continued to rock his body in an intoxicating rhythm.

His hands, handcuffed behind his back, prevented him for doing anything to loosen the tie anyway. An orgasm rip-roared through him. His tie totally closed around his throat, extinguishing *all* airflow. He expected it to release, but it did not.

Mitch's eyes bugged; he tossed his body from side to side. He battled, in vain, to dislodge the unyielding knot crushing his windpipe. The material only tightened. He wanted to shout – to beg for the tie to be loosened and removed. But he could only make futile popping and grunting sounds.

Just before he lost consciousness, excruciating pain shot from his genital area. A five-and-one-half-inch, boning knife slashed away at his testicles.

He rasped, taking his last, painful breath. Mitchell Peterson ceased to be.

* * * *

Just past noon, Roger and Scott arrived at a hotel off the Watterson Expressway. Christopher Hughes photographed a dead man's body and collected evidence. The maid had discovered this man.

A typical hotel room, it sported all the essentials: a sink, a shower, a low, particle board bureau with drawers, a fifteen-inch television, a king-sized bed, and a small nightstand with a phone atop.

The deceased lay on the bed, naked, other than a red tie around his neck. His hands were handcuffed behind his back. Scott recognized the man at once. *Mitchell Peterson*. "Son of a bitch!" he cursed. Being careful not to disrupt any evidence, he cautiously approached the foot of the bed.

Mitchell's face was bluish in color; his tongue protruded; his eyes grotesquely bulged. A pool of blood saturated the mattress, where a knife – the calling card to murder – maimed his testicles. If not for the knife, it might have merely appeared this man died of autoerotic hypoxia – engaging in sexual activity while restricting oxygen to the brain.

"Stacy did *not* do *this*," Scott proclaimed. "Give me motive for this one, Roger," he demanded, his face locked in a deep scowl.

"Maybe it's a copycat," Roger suggested, shrugging his shoulders.

On the same wavelength as Scott, he contemplated, *Stacy was just released on bail Friday. It's Saturday afternoon. Surely she did not leave jail to kill again.* This scenario did not sail with him either.

"Well, I can give you a suspect and a motive," Scott dared to reveal. Roger knew what his young partner was going to say. "Deputy Sheriff Jackson Charles Jordan. He hated Mitchell Peterson and wanted revenge. He's threatened both him and his wife on other occasions. In fact, we need to have someone check on Jeanette Peterson," Scott suggested.

"We have some short, red curly hairs again here too," Christopher volunteered, as he carefully bagged the evidence. "If it's a copycat, how'd they know about the hairs?"

"Can I get a warrant for a DNA sample from Deputy Jordan now, Roger?" Scott pushed.

"Why don't we let the evidence technicians finish their job, Scott? Then we'll discuss what warrants we might need and who we need to serve them on."

"We need to locate Jeanette Peterson," Scott proposed once more.

"I think that's a wise idea," Roger agreed. "Did the victim have a wallet?"

"Yes." Christopher answered. He opened his evidence box and pulled forth the wallet. He opened the plastic sack and pulled it forth. "Are you looking for his address?"

"Good guess," Roger smiled. "Yes."

"It's 5555 Walnutwood Road. I think that's in J-Town."

"It is," one of the LMPD officers chipped in. "I have a cousin that lives on that street. "It's right off Watterson Trail."

"Thanks, guys," Roger said. "Gather us some good evidence, Christopher."

"That's what I'm trying to do," he assured him.

* * * *

Roger and Scott drove to J-Town. Roger pulled his Impala in the driveway at 5555 Walnutwood Road. He pulled up close to the garage. Through the windows, a car could be seen.

"Well, there's a car in the garage," Roger commented, as he put the car in park and went to open his door.

Scott opened his door and vacated the car as well. They both walked up to the back door, which was closest to them. Roger knocked and rang the bell.

A few seconds later, they saw Jeanette Peterson walking across the kitchen toward them. She looked out through the window pane in the door, saw the two of them and recognized them, and unlocked the door, pulling it open. "Detectives," she addressed them. She looked flustered by their presence.

"Mrs. Peterson," Roger slowly began. He hated telling people one of their loved ones had died, but sometimes it was part of his job. He had relayed terrible news to families many times over the years. "I have some very bad news."

"What?" she asked. She physically braced herself against the door frame.

"I'm sorry to inform you that your husband has been murdered."

At hearing this information, Jeanette eyes opened wide. She placed a hand over her heart, inhaled a deep breath, and gasped, "Uhhhh!"

"We just came from the murder scene...a hotel off the Watterson," Roger further informed her.

"A h...hotel? Here in town?" she rattled off questions. "That...that's not possible," she contradicted. "Mitch...is out of town on business. You must have the wrong person."

"No, ma'am. I'm sorry. We don't. It's definitely your husband. He had identification on him," Roger confirmed.

"It was him," Scott concurred, chipping in for the first time. He had been quietly analyzing Jeanette's reaction to their news.

"When's the last time you saw your husband?" Roger asked.

"Um...God...this can't be happening!" Jeanette proclaimed, instead of answering Roger's question. She lowered her head, placed her hand over her mouth, and closed her eyes. She seemed very close to a meltdown.

"Why don't we go inside and have a seat?" Roger suggested. He reached out and grabbed her shoulder to turn her.

Jeanette opened her eyes and dropped her hand down from her face. "Oh, I…I'm sorry. I should have invited you in…" she began to apologize.

"That's okay, ma'am," Roger excused her. "I know you are shocked by our news. I just thought it might be easier if we talked sitting down."

"Yeah. My legs are a little weak," she professed. Jeanette turned then and led them inside. The last one in, Scott turned and shut the back door. They walked over to a small wooden table in the middle of the room.

Scott glanced around. *A typical kitchen*, he absently thought. *A refrigerator, stove, microwave, kitchen sink, and wood cabinets.* Shiny, neutral colored tile graced the floor. A cloudy day outside, the room needed additional illumination, so Jeanette hit the wall switch, turning on the globe light on the ceiling fan overhead. They all had a seat at the table.

"My…my daughter…is taking a nap," she explained in a shaky voice.

"Do you think we will disturb her if we talk in here?" Roger considerately asked.

"No. Susanna sleeps like a log. She's a wonderful child," Jeanette bragged, a smile coming to her face. She obviously adored the little girl. "God…first Renee commits suicide, almost a year ago. And now…this! I'm all Susanna has," Jeanette proclaimed. She dropped her head into her hands and kneaded her forehead with her fingers.

Roger and Scott waited for the tears and sobbing to begin. But when Jeanette lowered her hands from her face, dry, glassy eyes greeted them. She appeared to be in shock. Roger did not find this reaction all that strange.

Hysterical reactions followed actually seeing a dead body – as in the maid at the hotel that had discovered Mitch's dead body. Witnesses gave account of her running down the corridors, crying, screaming in Spanish, and wildly waving her arms.

On the other hand, the last time Jeanette saw her husband he had been alive and well. Hearing otherwise was probably surreal for her right now. "Jeanette, can you please tell us the last time you saw your husband?" Roger revisited his earlier question.

"Yesterday morning," she answered. She stared straight ahead, and her voice was expressionless. "We had breakfast together. Mitch went to work. I left to take Susanna to daycare, and then I headed to work. Mitch was supposed to have flown to Pittsburgh yesterday for some sales conference. He was supposed to get home Sunday evening."

"When's the last time the two of you spoke?"

"He...he called me at five to say he was heading to the airport. He had an eight o'clock flight. I haven't heard from him since, but I didn't think anything about it. His flight got in late, and he was supposed to be in meetings today... What on earth was he doing at a hotel, here in town?" she asked. The news of his death finally sinking in, tears came to her eyes now.

"We're not sure," Roger told her.

"H...how did he...did he...die?" she fought to ask, sheepishly looking into Roger's eyes.

"He was strangled to death," Roger replied.

"Oh my God! How horrible!" Jeanette shrieked, dropping her head into her hands again. Her shoulders did begin to shake now, and they could hear her sobbing. She seemed to be appalled and brokenhearted.

Roger and Scott patiently waited for her emotional breakdown to subside. It took several moments before Jeanette regained her composure. When she raised her head, she looked at both men with bloodshot eyes and stuttered, "Who…who…" She sounded like an owl.

Roger and Scott waited for her to finish her sentence. Although, Roger had a good idea what she was trying to ask. *She wants to know who did this to her husband.*

She completed his thought a second later. "Who did this?" she asked.

"We don't know yet," Roger confessed.

"When *will* you know?" she pushed. Her grief seemed to be turning to anger now.

"As soon as we've processed all the evidence we found at the crime scene," Roger replied.

"What evidence?" she probed. Her eyes intently studied him now.

"I don't know yet," Roger was deliberately vague. "Our evidence technicians were processing the crime scene when we left to come and inform you of the news. I'll be honest with you, Mrs. Peterson…"

"Please call me Jeanette," she requested. "We will be talking a lot. I want to know everything you find out about my husband's murder," she told them, alert and coherent again.

"Okay…Jeanette…the truth is…we won't have answers for you for at least a month or more…"

"A month or more!" she repeated, sounding incredulous. "Why so long?"

"Depending on what our techs find, we may have to have some DNA testing done. The labs are backed up, even the private ones we use here in the city. We need these results back to help us piece together the puzzle of who murdered your husband."

"You need to question Deputy Jordan," Jeanette strongly suggested, all at once. "He threatened both me and Mitch. He had Mitch arrested for hitting him at the Judicial Center, after he was spreading lies about me. He's crazy," she professed.

Scott suddenly tuned in. He wanted to question Deputy Jordan as well. Not content with ignoring his suspicions, he still believed Jack had a hand in Renee's death and could have in Chad's and Debbie's as well. *If he already killed three people, what would one more matter – especially a man he hated?*

"Jeanette, we may question Deputy Jordan, if the evidence warrants us doing so," Roger assured her.

"He ran his mouth with lies about me, and Mitch defended my honor and got thrown in jail. Would you question him, or would it be a cover-up, since he's one of you guys?"

"It doesn't matter if he's a law enforcement officer or not," Roger tried to convince her. "Deputy Jordan *will* be questioned, just like anyone else, if the evidence warrants us doing so."

"We will question him," Scott chipped in again with determination, very eager for the evidence to make itself to the lab. If any part of it suggested a man had a hand in this crime, he would push for Deputy Jordan to be questioned.

"You better, because I won't let this die," Jeanette threatened. "I want the person punished that did this to my husband," she demanded.

Me too! Scott determined. *Especially if the same person is responsible for Debbie's death. I'll see to it that the killer rots in jail, even if it is Deputy Jack Jordan*, he vowed.

* * * *

Since the MO of the crime seemed to be the exact same as the last two homicides, the DNA evidence was dropped off at the Chamberlain Lane lab once again. Looking more and more like a serial killer on the loose, the investigative team needed to get results as quickly as possible.

A little quiet as he received in this evidence, Mickey Charles accepted this murder to be very similar in nature to the other homicides he worked on of late. It seemed to be a direct tie-in with the Chad Kennison and Debbie Gray murders. He had felt guilty when Debbie Gray had been murdered in the same manner as Chad Kennison, but evidence technicians came up blank on gathering hard evidence in that murder.

At this murder scene, short, curly, red hairs had been gathered. Vaginal secretions and saliva samples also comprised some of the evidence. If DNA from any of these substances came back belonging to a male, Mickey would have to let the findings stand. He could not allow a serial killer to run loose and to continue to kill. Not even for Darry – not even to avenge an old score for Mary.

Chapter 26

Leaving Kentucky

As always, he reflected with elation on his latest kill. When he made the suggestion to meet at a hotel for a night of hot, kinky sex, Mitch leaped at the chance. Mitchell Peterson never turned down an offer of sex. Mitch sickened him.

When he handcuffed Mitch's hands behind his back, Mitch only smiled. *He also slapped me on the bottom. "Bad!" I chastised...but laughed in welcome. I slowly undressed him then.*

He quivered now as he pictured placing the red tie around Mitch's bare neck. "What's the tie for?" Mitch asked. "Are we playing fuck the banker?"

"Something like that," he answered with a snicker. "You know they say if you cut off airflow right before an orgasm, it makes it ten times greater. Would you like to find out?"

Mitch looked ambivalent about this idea. *So I disrobed, fondled and kissed Mitch's erection. Mitch changed his mind very quickly after that, becoming game for anything I suggested.*

I couldn't decide whether to make the killing look like all the others or not. If I only strangled Mitch to death during sex, it would look like an accident. But where is the fun in that? In the end, he decided he wanted to leave his mark.

As Mitch entered the troughs of orgasm, I pushed the slipknot on the tie hard into his trachea. Mitch struggled to take in air; his eyes pleaded for the tie to be loosened. He tried to talk, but could only make broken, high-pitched noises. He sounded rather like a dolphin or a bird. *Instead of loosening the tie, I pushed it as tight as it would go.*

When Mitch realized the tie would not be released, he began to thrash about. *I stood at the foot of the bed and watched him struggle. It was so fulfilling.*

I retrieved the knife. I held it up so Mitch could see it. Then, as he kicked his legs, I sank it into his precious family jewels. It had given him great satisfaction to slash away at Mitchell's prized manhood before he died.

Mitch sharply inhaled, wheezing, and then his body went limp. *This punishment was just what Mitch deserved. Mitch was scum!*

Now, with Mitch dead, another important decision needed to be made. *Should I stay in Kentucky or leave the state?*

Charged with Chad Kennison's murder, and looked at in the Debbie Gray murder as well, Stacy Prescott would likely be suspect in this latest murder too. Having gotten away with several murders, he knew better than to push his luck. *Get out while the getting is good.*

If he left Kentucky and went to another state, he could always kill again there, if the desire to do so raised its tempting head. It would be harder to link murders in another state to the string of murders he had already committed. Moving made logical sense. Currently, he breathed easier just knowing Mitchell Peterson counted among the deceased.

Could Mitchell be my final kill? Is so, he could stay in the area. *But killing is such fun. I get such a rise from it. Do I really want to quit?* The answers to these questions would determine whether he left state of stayed. He intended to give it considerable, serious thought.

Chapter 27

After the Murder

Monday morning, Roger and Scott paid a visit to Deputy Jordan to find out his whereabouts the night of Mitchell Peterson's death. He expected them. Charly had relayed the news about Mitchell Peterson's death, after Jeanette called in and told her. As expected, Jeanette had also indicated she would be spending the day making funeral arrangements.

"Look, first thing, you keep that young prick out of my face," Jack addressed Roger, pointing a finger at Scott and staring holes through him. Scott averted his eyes and remained silent. He did not want to arouse Jack's ire. He had been warned by Roger to keep a low profile.

"Not a problem," Roger guaranteed. "Can we go someplace private and talk?"

They stood on the second floor, just outside of Charly and Jeanette's offices. Jack had been in the office talking to Charly.

"We can go in the Jury Assembly Hall if you'd like. There's a workroom in the back with a door that closes. The jurors won't be there until 9:00. It's 8:10 now, so we have plenty of time. I'm not expecting our conversation will be long." Plainly unhappy about Roger and Scott being there, Jack had an edge to his voice.

"No. Our conversation should not take long at all," Roger replied.

Jack led the way into the Jury Assembly Hall and to the workroom in the back. The last one in the room, Scott closed the door. Jack sat in a chair close to the door on the right-hand side of the long table. Roger sat in the chair at the end, and Scott sat across from Jack. Jack still glared at Scott, so he looked down at the shiny table top.

"Jack, I appreciate you taking a few moments for us this morning," Roger cordially began. "We'll be brief and to the point…"

"I know what you want to know. You guys think I had something to do with Mitchell Peterson's death, because there was bad blood between us…"

"And did you?" Roger wasted no time asking. Jack had thrown them into this conversation. Roger would have eased into it otherwise.

"No. I did not!" he firmly maintained. "I'm not sorry the guy is dead. I'll honestly admit that. He was a real scum bucket. This world is better without him in it, but I was not the one to take him out."

"No offense, Jack. But it sounds like you hated the man," Roger pointed out.

"I did," Jack confessed, gripping the edge the table. "I hate Jeanette too. She's a cold bitch. If anyone close to Mitchell might have killed him, you should look in her direction. I'm still not sure, since my handcuffs ended up with Renee, she didn't have something to do with her death."

"We're not looking in any real direction yet," Roger tried to assure him. "All we wanted to know was where you were Friday night."

"Friday, I was home in my apartment all evening and night," Jack answered.

"Alone?"

"Yes."

"So no one can verify you were there."

"My word as a fellow officer of the law should do that," he reminded Roger. He looked Roger square in the eye, as if he should understand this fact. "As much as I hate to admit I share space on this earth with certain people, it's still my job to protect people and not to take them out."

"True," Roger agreed. "So the last time you saw Mitchell Peterson…?"

"Was the day he slugged me, and I had him arrested."

"Haven't you wanted revenge for that day?" Roger questioned.

"I got my revenge the right way, by having him arrested. I haven't seen him since. It's kept him out of this building and out of my face. I wish I could say the same about Mitchell's wife, Jeanette, but I have to see her each day because she works here. We only communicate when we need to, and it will remain that way."

"That would be a good thing, Jack. Trouble between you and Jeanette Peterson would not look too good right now," Roger cautioned.

"Don't I know it. I have no doubt you guys are questioning me today because Jeanette pointed the finger at me. I'm telling you guys, you'd be wise to look in her direction instead."

The two are still accusing each other, Scott noted. He had witnessed this back and forth allegation the day he questioned them both about Renee's death – the day Mitchell Peterson struck Jack and got arrested. Scott considered either of them to still be a worthy suspect. But since the unknown DNA was male, Jack still rang a more likely candidate than Jeanette. *For now.*

"Jack, as I said, we appreciate your time," Roger said, rising to his feet.

Scott pushed his chair back and stood as well. He regretted the interrogation of Deputy Jack had ended, but they garnered all the information they were going to for now. Until the DNA results came back from the crime scene, they would be at a standstill.

When these results came back, perhaps Scott could talk Roger into getting a warrant to gather DNA from Jack. After all, Jack presented no solid alibi for the night of Mitchell's murder. Once they tested Jack's DNA, they would know, once and for all, whether this man had a hand in any of the murders or not. For now, they would have to play the waiting game.

They all vacated the conference room, walked through the assembly hall and out into the hallway. They went their separate directions.

* * * *

The day after her husband's burial, Jeanette called Roger. "So have you gotten any closer to finding my husband's killer?" she asked.

"No. Not yet," he informed her. "I will let you know as soon as we know anything. All of the DNA evidence found at the murder scene has been sent to the lab. So as soon as the results come back, I will have a better idea which direction to look in."

"So there was DNA evidence?" Jeanette inquired. "What kind?"

"Some hairs and some bodily fluids," Roger disclosed. "As I said, we'll know more once we have the DNA results."

"Have you talked to Deputy Jordan?" she pushed.

"Yes, we did," Roger told her.

"And?"

"And…as of now, we have no evidence putting him at the scene of your husband's murder. As I said, DNA evidence might tell us otherwise…if it comes back male. If it comes back female, we will, of course, be looking at Stacy Prescott again, since the MO was the same in Mitchell's murder as in Chad Kennison's."

"Do you really think Stacy Prescott killed Mitchell? Why?"

"I don't know the answers to your questions, Jeanette. At least not yet. You'll need to give us more time."

"Okay," she agreed with some hesitation, impatient for answers. Her agitation seemed normal for a grieving wife.

"I promise we will call you the second we know anything," Roger vowed.

"Alright," she agreed again. "I'll be in touch," she said. The serious tone of her voice suggested, *I'll be watching you.*

Roger hung up the phone then. Seeing Scott looking at him, he said, "Jeanette Peterson. She wanted to know if we knew anything about her husband's murder yet."

"Sounds pretty typical," Scott commented. "Everyone watches CSI on television and thinks detectives have an answer immediately – after the commercial break. It's a shame it can't really be that fast." He still agonized over not having more answers in Debbie's homicide.

"Yes, it is," Roger agreed. He picked up some paperwork on his desk and began to study it. He saw no use in beleaguering over Jeanette's call, until they had some evidence in hand to lead them one way or another.

Scott still pondered her call though. *Either she's a grieving widow who wants justice or a murderer who wants to know if we are on her trail.* He wanted evidence in hand as badly as Roger, maybe even more, especially if this murder tied into Debbie's. He tried to concentrate on work as well.

At work, he was fine. But when alone, the pain of Debbie's death still stung like a wasp. He missed her terribly. He had to find answers and bring someone to justice for her murder. He would not rest until he did.

Chapter 28

DNA Samples

A month and a half later, the DNA results came back from the Chamberlain Lane lab. The semen sample matched Mitchell Peterson's DNA, as did the blood. The red hairs and other bodily fluid matched to an unknown male. This male DNA also matched to the unidentified male DNA found at the Chad Kennison murder scene.

Scott went ballistic when he read the report. "All of the DNA evidence points to a male suspect, even the bodily fluid the evidence technician thought was vaginal fluid. Now do you agree I have probable cause to order DNA testing of Deputy Sheriff Jack Jordan?" he pushed. He stood beside Roger's desk, lording over him, waving the folder with the DNA results in his partner's face.

Roger gritted his teeth, shook his head, and rubbed the bridge of his nose. He did not want to concede to testing Jack Jordan, but for once, he agreed with Scott. They did have probable cause to consider him a suspect now: Two pairs of his handcuffs found at the site of Renee Peterson's death; Jack's flaming, wavy red hair; his angry outrage with the world in general; his ready accessibility to all of the victims; a strong, unresolved, angry grudge against Mitchell Peterson; and no confirmable alibi the night of Mitchell's death.

"Okay," he approved, puckering his lips and loudly exhaling.

He picked up the phone to start the channels flowing on obtaining a warrant to gather a DNA sample from Deputy Sheriff Jackson Charles Jordan. Roger hoped testing Deputy Jordan's DNA advanced their case. If not, they might end up with egg on their faces, but the evidence warranted the search. He did not want a killer to go free any more than Scott did.

* * * *

Roger went over to the Hall of Justice to get his warrant. Christopher Hughes met him at the Judicial Center. Scott stayed at the office. Already too much bad blood between Scott and Jack, Roger did not want an angry confrontation at the Judicial Center if it could somehow be avoided. Jack would not be happy about this search anyway, but he might take it better from Roger than Scott. At least Roger hoped so.

Roger approached the other deputy sheriffs watching the door. "Excuse me, do you, by chance, know where Deputy Jordan might be?" he asked.

A woman deputy answered, "He's up in the Jury Pool Assembly Hall. They're picking some potential jurors, and he'll walk them to the assigned courtroom."

"Okay. Thanks," Roger answered.

He and Christopher headed to the stairway. Roger preferred elevators, but he did not want to wait on one. He wanted to confront Jack now, if possible. If Jack went into one of the courtrooms, Roger might have to wait to serve the warrant on him. He wanted to get this unpleasantness over as soon as possible.

As Roger and Christopher rounded the stairs at the top, they looked into the Jury Assembly Hall through the glass wall. Jeanette stood at the podium, talking into a handheld microphone. She called potential jurors. The prospects vacated chairs and came to stand beside Deputy Jack in the front of the room by the door.

Roger and Christopher opened the glass door and entered the room. Roger said, "Excuse me" to a few of the jurors surrounding Jack and pushed his way forward toward Jack. Christopher also made his way through these people, following at Roger's heel.

Jeanette noticed the slight disruption beside her. She glanced over and saw two men approach Jack. She recognized the older man – *Detective Roger Matthews*. She stopped announcing juror numbers for a second and gave full attention to the scenario unfolding beside her.

"Jack, we need to talk to you for a moment," she heard Roger say.

"Gentlemen, is there a problem?" she asked, briefly turning the microphone off.

"What business is that of yours?" Jack snapped in his usual hostile voice.

"A lot, if this has anything to do with Mitchell's death," she told him, giving him a stare cold enough to freeze.

"Is that why you're here? Does this have something to do with Mitchell Peterson's death?" Jack asked Roger.

"Yes. It does," Roger honestly replied.

"You've got to fuckin' be kidding," Jack declared, shaking his head.

Jeanette struggled not to smile.

"This will only take a second, Jack. Can you step outside with us?"

The jurors standing all around them watched and looked back and forth amongst one another. Roger did not want to embarrass Jack in front of them. He would have preferred for what little conversation had already taken place not to have.

"Look, I told you everything I know about Mitchell Peterson's death the day you guys questioned me. I'm working here. I don't have time for unnecessary interruptions."

"Well, you are going to have to take the time," Roger informed him. "I have a warrant to collect some DNA from you," he said in a quiet voice. Roger hoped they did not have to, but they would do it right in the midst of all these people if Jack forced them to.

"Son of a bitch!" he cursed. "I never thought I'd see the day! My own people are turning against me. Are you going to take a DNA sample from Jeanette as well?"

"We have no cause to," Roger answered.

"And you actually think you have cause to with me?" Jack inquired. He looked up at the ceiling in frustration, shaking his head some more.

"Jack, can we get on with this, please?" Roger requested.

He allowed Christopher to step in front of him. Christopher sat his case on the floor, snapped it open and pulled forth a cotton swab. "Can you open your mouth for me, Deputy Jordan?" Christopher asked.

"What's this little punk rocker have to do with anything?" Jack asked with loathing, glaring at Christopher spiked hair and looking over his shoulder at Roger.

"I'm an LMPD Evidence Technician," Christopher told Jack. "Will you open your mouth for me, please, so I can gather a DNA sample?" *Other than that, you can shut it!* Christopher mused with hostility. *This guy is a real piece of work. He's certainly opinionated and seems mad at the world.*

"Unbelievable! Just goes to show they will let anything on the force these days," he criticized. Jack defiantly crossed his arms across his chest, but he dropped his mouth open as requested.

Christopher swabbed the inside of his mouth. Then he placed the swab into a closed container and stored the sample in his case. "Thank you," he said. He turned and began making his way through the crowd of potential jurors. Still all eyes, they whispered amongst themselves now, obviously discussing what just transpired.

"That's all for now, Jack," Roger explained, as he too turned to leave.

"You guys should be ashamed of yourself!" Jack yelled after them. Roger ignored him and kept walking. He regretted having to take DNA from a fellow officer, and part of him hoped it came back not being a match. But another part of him wanted to catch a serial killer. And if the DNA matched, fellow officer or not, Deputy Jordan would be arrested.

* * * *

Before Roger got back to the office, Scott received an agitated call from Jeanette. "Your partner just collected a DNA sample from Deputy Jordan. What is up with that? Do you have evidence linking him to Mitchell's murder?" she fired questions.

Pleased to hear from Jeanette, he surprised her when he said, "I'd like to come over and talk to you about what we have so far. Can you meet me in the Hall of Justice dining area? I'll buy you a soft drink."

"If the talk has to do with finding Mitch's killer, then of course, I can meet you," Jeanette agreed.

"Okay. I'll meet you there in a few minutes," Scott concluded, hanging up the phone. *Perfect!* he thought with glee, as he tossed his suit jacket over his shoulder and headed out.

* * * *

In the dining area at the Hall of Justice, several men and women, lawyers, potential jurors, and deputy sheriffs, whisk past Scott. Not paying any attention to any of them, Scott focused on the task at hand – getting a sample of Jeanette's DNA.

As he saw her approach, he headed toward a nearby table. Scott suggested, "Have a seat. What would you like to drink? Like I said, I'll buy you a soft drink."

"Um…I usually drink Pepsi," Jeanette rather absently answered. Not interested in drinking something, she only wished to know what information Scott had to share.

"Have a seat. I'll be right back," Scott instructed.

Before Jeanette could object, his long legs carried him around the corner to the food vendors. He stepped up to the one selling burgers and such and ordered two Pepsis. He requested lots of ice in one of them – more ice, less soda. It only took the man behind the counter a few seconds to fill up two sixteen ounce cups with ice and soda. He placed them on the counter in front of Scott and told him the cost: "$2.12".

Scott handed the man three dollars. "Just keep the change," he told him. In a hurry to get back to Jeanette, Scott cared nothing about a few coins. He grabbed the cups and retrieved a straw for Jeanette's drink.

Coming back to the table, Scott sat Jeanette's drink and straw in front of her on the table. Sitting down, with his drink still in hand, he popped the lid off of his cup. He took a small drink, and then he sat his cup on the table.

Scott watched, in anticipation, as Jeanette tapped the end of her straw on the table, shoving the other end through the paper. She slipped the straw loose from the paper cover, and she thrush it through the plastic lid on her soft drink.

Oblivious to anything, or anyone, else in the room, Scott's eyes followed the movement of Jeanette's arm as she picked up the blue Pepsi cup and placed the straw in her mouth. *Ericka!* His brain registered with joy as her lips touched the straw. *DNA in the making. And without the hassle of getting a warrant.*

Getting a warrant in Jeanette's case would have been difficult, if not next to impossible, since crime scene DNA pointed them in the direction of a male suspect. Scott still wanted Jeanette's DNA tested just as a precaution. In his mind, too much suspicion pointed her way to not have her tested as well. *Perhaps she underwent a sex change.* As unlikely as this theory appeared, anything could be possible.

Having taken a good-sized drink, Jeanette sat the cup back on the table. "So are you going to tell me what you've found out so far about Mitch's killer?" she demanded, frowning with annoyance. She also squeezed the side of her cup.

"Yeah. Of course," Scott agreed, picking his soft drink back up and pouring a bit more down his throat. "We got the DNA results back today," Scott explained. "It tells us we are looking for a male suspect. We don't know for certain if that male suspect is Jack or not. That's why we took a sample of his DNA. Who else did your husband know that had short, curly, red hair? That is...other than...*you*?" Scott added, deliberately staring at Jeanette's hair. He wanted her to notice him looking.

Without thinking, she reached to finger a few strands of her hair.

I touched a nerve, Scott concluded with satisfaction.

Noticing Scott's scrutiny, Jeanette released her hair and lowered her arm. She still squeezed her cup with her other hand. She had not taken another drink. "My husband... Mitch...was an investment banker. He had to meet with an abundance of people on a regular basis. I don't know of anyone in particular that had red hair, but I'm sure he knew some redheaded men. I don't know why anyone would want to hurt him though…other than Jack. Couldn't it have been a stranger, as well? It obviously wasn't Stacy Prescott, because you are looking for a *man*, and she is a woman."

She's stressing that we are looking for a man. She wants to take suspicion off women. That includes herself. "That's right. We *are* looking for a man," Scott agreed, a strange smile of his face. He observed her drinking some more of her soda.

"So is that it? That's all you have to tell me? All I can say is I'm glad you took a DNA sample from Deputy Jordan. He hated us both. He still hates me. He tried to slander me again today. He asked your partner if he was going to take a DNA sample from me as well. As if I would have something to do with my husband's death. Jack is crazy," Jeanette accused, sounding a bit hostile. She took another few draws of Pepsi.

"We're looking at anyone who has short, curly, red hair who had contact with Mitch," Scott disclosed, carefully perusing her reaction.

Jeanette pulled the straw from her mouth and met his eyes with puzzled eyes. "You mean any *man* who has short, curly, red hair. You said the DNA was male, right?"

"Yeah. That's right," he concurred. "But people aren't always what they seem."

"What's that supposed to mean?" Jeanette asked, sitting her cup back down on the table.

Scott caught a slight tremor in her hand. *She's nervous.* "I just mean even a woman could be a suspect. You take you, for instance…how do I know for certain you are really a woman? You look like a woman. But so does someone who's had…say…a sex change…"

"What? That's the most ridiculous thing I've ever heard!" she declared. Her eyes darted up and to the side, and she brought her hand up to stroke her lower lip.

199

Her eye movements and body language tell me she is nervous and possibly lying, Scott deduced with pleasure. He gave a fake chuckle. "Sounds that way, doesn't it? But the only way to know for certain would be for you to take a DNA test. You wouldn't mind giving me a DNA sample, would you?"

"No. Of course I wouldn't," she vowed, but her eyes continued to look upward and to the side, and she slightly gnawed at her lip now. "You're not actually asking me to give you one, are you?"

"It would be no big deal if I was, right?" Scott pushed.

"I told you it wouldn't. But it would be a waste of time. I'm *not* a man!" she strongly professed.

"Of course you aren't," Scott agreed with a deceptive grin. No purpose would be served in spooking Jeanette. "We kind of got off on a tangent here. I'm sorry. I only came over to tell you about the DNA results we have so far. I thought you might like to talk face-to-face," he lied.

"Oh...I appreciate that," Jeanette answered, relaxing a little. She met Scott's eyes again. "I probably should be getting back to work though."

Jeanette picked up her drink. As she sucked through the straw, Scott heard a familiar 'sluuurp' and knew Jeanette's cup was empty. As she took the straw out of her mouth and sat the cup back on the table, Scott stood, reached across the table, and picked up her drink.

Seeing Jeanette give him a strange look, he asked, "You were finished, weren't you?"

"Yes," she replied, pushing her chair back and standing as well.

"Okay. I'll throw this away for you," Scott told her. "We'll be in touch. We aren't giving up on finding your husband's killer. In fact, we are dedicated to finding the killer;

we are going to do whatever it takes to find this individual. This *person* will be brought to justice. You can take that to the bank."

"Okay. Thanks," Jeanette replied. She suddenly seemed preoccupied.

"See ya later," Scott said, concluding their conversation. He headed off toward the nearest trash can. He watched as Jeanette quickly headed away in the opposite direction. She did not look back in his direction. Scott cautiously slid the straw from her cup. He pulled a plastic evidence bag out of his suit jacket. He dropped the straw inside, sealed the bag, and stashed his gathering back inside his jacket pocket. He walked off with an enormous, satisfied smile across his face. *Mission accomplished.*

* * * *

Scott went to his car and drove to the Chamberlain Lane lab. He asked to speak to Mickey Charles. A few minutes later, Mickey came out of the lab. "Can I help you?" he asked.

"Hi. I'm Detective Scott Arnold," Scott introduced himself, offering his hand.

Mickey shook his hand. "What can I do for you today, Detective Arnold?" he asked.

Scott reached in his pocket and pulled forth the evidence bag. "I need some more DNA testing done in the Mitchell Peterson case."

"So it ties in with the handcuff slasher case?" Mickey asked. This description had been coined by the media.

"Yes. It does," Scott agreed.

"I'll see that the testing on this, and the other DNA brought in a little earlier, is moved to the top of the line. But, still at best, it will take a few weeks."

"I'll take it," Scott agreed. "Whatever you can do to speed up the process I will appreciate."

"If it helps get a serial killer off the street, then I'm happy to do it," Mickey agreed. He reached through heavy, wiry, black hair on the side of his head to scratch. He was thinking, *If I can right the wrong I did when I changed results on the first murder, it will be worth it to see a rush order put on this request.*

"Thanks again," Scott said as he turned to leave.

"No problem," Mickey said again.

The two parted. Scott could hardly wait for a few weeks to pass. He would wait until he had the results of the DNA testing in hand before he shared with Roger what he had done. This way, if Jeanette's DNA did not match, Roger would not be in an uproar, and tell Scott he was wasting time. But if they did come back a match, Roger would finally have to eat crow. Scott almost prayed Jeanette's DNA matched.

* * * *

When Darrell heard DNA had been obtained from Deputy Jordan, he called Mickey. "We had a Deputy Sheriff's DNA collected in the Mitchell Peterson case," he informed his friend. "What's going on? I take it you provided LMPD detectives with male DNA."

"I had to, Darry," Mickey answered with regret. "A single murder is one thing. But it looks as if a serial killer is on the loose. I can't allow this guy, whoever he is, to go on killing."

"But, Mickey, I've got Stacy Prescott going to trial in a little over a month."

"I know. And since the evidence in the Chad Kennison murder mostly matches to her, maybe you'll get a conviction."

"But if other crimes with the same MO have a different murder suspect, it provide a jury reasonable doubt. Stacy may walk," Darrell pointed out with disenchantment.

"Maybe you can make the case for some type of conspiracy between the male suspect and Stacy," Mickey suggested.

"I wish you could have helped me out again with this latest murder," Darrell told him.

"Me too, Darry. But I can't allow a serial killer to go free and keep on killing. You don't want that either. At the very least, Stacy and her family are being made to sweat for a while. That should give you some gratification."

"Yeah. I guess it will have to," Darrell said, deflated.

"Sorry, Darry. I did all I could."

"Okay, pal," Darrell condoned, grateful for what help Mickey had provided him. "Don't sweat it. I appreciate what you did do."

"I hope Stacy still gets punished," Mickey admitted.

"I'll do my best to see she is," Darrell promised. "You take care."

"You too, Darry," Mickey said.

Their conversation concluded. Darrell lamented Mickey's decision not to tamper with evidence on this latest murder. But he understood why his friend had not. *Mickey's right. We can't allow a serial killer to roam free on the streets of Louisville. I'll just have to try and make a case against both Stacy and this unknown man. I'd like to see them both pay. Conspiracy – that's a pretty good thought. Maybe I can go with this angle. I'll have to see, once the detectives uncover who our male murderer is. I hope I can find a way to tie Stacy to this person.*

Darrell wanted revenge on the Prescott's so badly he could taste it. Framing Stacy Prescott for Chad's murder had seemed the perfect way to enact his revenge, but now, he needed to put back on his Commonwealth's Attorney hat and punish the real killer as well. Darrell hoped he could have his cake and eat it too – get revenge on the Prescott's and punish the real killer. He would focus all of his efforts on making this dream a reality.

Chapter 30

Moving On

With a permanent marker, he labeled **Kitchen Items** on the box he had just packed. Several other boxes formed stacks against an empty wall in the living room. He had been packing for a while, ever since the notion of moving occurred to him.

Suspicion and accusation by the police provided the straw that broke the camel's back. Even though the police had no case against him, he did not wish to press his luck. If they continued to look long and hard enough, they might eventually find something linking him to the murders. He had used care each time, perpetrating the perfect crimes – or so he thought. But evidently, his *perfect* crimes left a lot to be desired. The homicide squad had gathered evidence at the murder sites. *It's time to move on*, he decided. He pulled out another box to pack some more items.

* * * *

The day after Roger took a DNA sample from Jack, he filed papers to begin his retirement process. Working in Kentucky had begun to stink for him.

Friday, November 1, Jack Jordan worked his last day as a Jefferson County Deputy Sheriff. His fellow deputies at the Judicial Center threw a surprise retirement party for him. One of the courtrooms acted as the party center; banners, streamers, and balloons hung about the room. A large sheet cake resided on a long table by the wall. A punchbowl full of an orange sherbet and ginger ale mix sat beside the cake. A tablecloth, paper cups, plates and napkins, with Happy Retirement on them, also adorned the table.

Wall-to-wall deputy sheriffs filled the room. Several judges and lawyers, who had known Jack for years, also attended. In fact, one of the judges provided the ruse needed to get Jack to the courtroom for the party. He said he needed to meet with him there.

Thoroughly surprised when he entered the courtroom, a boisterous "Surprise!" shouted by all in the room added to the excitement for Jack. For the first time in years, he felt appreciated. The nice gifts, and reminiscent speeches, presented to him by many, including Charly and Amy from the Jury Administrator's office, also gave Jack the warm fuzzies.

Afterwards, directed to cut the cake, Jack picked up the cake server and carved out a piece of chocolate cake. After he took the first slice, nearly everyone else in the room stepped to fill plates with cake for themselves. They also filled cups with punch.

After eating some cake and drinking some punch, Charly dropped into a long line, folks waiting to approach Jack and wish him a fond farewell. She eventually got her turn. "Jack, we are going to miss you," she told him, engulfing him in a hug.

When she pulled back, she slipped her glasses off for a second and dabbed at her eyes with a tissue. She liked Jack a great deal and was truly going to miss him.

"Thanks, Charly. I will miss you as well. But I won't miss your partner," he did not fail to add. His words spewed hostility.

"Jeanette is off sick today," Charly shared.

"Oh…and I'm sure if she wasn't, she would have been here. Then again, maybe she would have – to celebrate. She'll be glad to be rid of me."

"I'm sorry there has been bad blood between the two of you, Jack. You're a good man."

"Yes, I am," he professed with vanity. "All I've ever done I've done to improve the world."

"I believe that," Charly agreed, giving him a bittersweet smile. "I wish you all the best, Jack."

"Thanks, Charly. I wish the same for you," he professed, giving her another slight hug.

He would miss people like Charly, but he welcomed getting away from people like Jeanette. He also delighted in getting away from the likes of Detective Scott Arnold and his infuriating suspicions.

Bye Kentucky. Hello, new life.

* * * *

He loaded up a U-Haul truck with all of the boxes it would hold. Professional movers would move big items – furniture and appliances. He had already taken several boxes of his possessions to a nearby DAV. Simplifying his life, he discarded everything but items he deemed absolutely necessary. A fresh start awaited him in another state, and he could hardly wait.

He climbed into the cab of the truck, started it up, and drove away, heading down the road to his new future.

Chapter 31

Truth

Scott held the findings from the DNA testing in his hands. It had taken three weeks to get these results. Fingering the flap of the envelope for a few moments, he allowed his nerves to settle. He badly wanted a match to the crime DNA they had collected.

He took a deep breath and ripped opened the manila envelope. Pulling the contents loose, his eyes quickly scanned the written report. Disappointment washed over Scott as he discovered one of their suspects did *not* match. He lowered the pages for a second.

Gathering his courage, he raised the pages again a few moments later. He read on, despite the fact that he did not expect the other suspect to be a match either. Scott's heart accelerated, as this assumption proved wrong. The other suspect positively matched. Exuberant, Scott declared out loud, "Yes!" An adrenaline rush also had him doing a small, delighted dance.

"Scott looks happy," he heard Abe proclaim and looked over his shoulder to see Abe and his partner staring and laughing at him.

"Ohhh…yeah!" Scott agreed. "Happy is an understatement. I'm ecstatic, gentlemen!" he shared, cackling and giving them a gaping smile.

Scott sprung into his desk chair. He snatched up the phone receiver to call Darrell. "Indictment time!" he practically sang, as he dialed.

Scott hated that Roger was not there. He was out to lunch. He could hardly wait to share his happy news with him. *Debbie, your death will be avenged. And so will yours, Renee. I knew you didn't commit suicide. I may not be able to prove this, but we have enough evidence to send your killer away for a good while – for at least one murder: your husband, Mitchell.*

"Darrell Prescott," Scott heard the Commonwealth Attorney answer.

"Darrell, this is Detective Arnold. I have some wonderful news," Scott shared, getting on with the business at hand. The quicker he shared his news with Darrell, the quicker he would have his arrest warrant. Scott could hardly wait.

* * * *

Scott barely lowered the receiver when another call came in. "Homicide Division, Detective Arnold," he answered.

"Detective Arnold, this is Charly Donaldson from the Judicial Center," she informed him.

"Hello, Ms. Donaldson, what can I do for you today?" Scott asked. He found it an odd coincidence she had called. He had intended to make a visit to the Judicial Center – one, to apologize to the innocent, whose DNA did *not* match, and two, to question the presumed killer, whose DNA *did* match.

"Well…I hate to bother you guys…but…I'm a bit concerned…"

"About what?" Scott questioned.

"About Jeanette," Charly revealed. "She called in sick Friday. I thought maybe she was just doing this to avoid Jack's retirement celebration…"

"Jack retired?" Scott inquired with noted surprise.

"Yes. You guys having suspicions about him embarrassed him, and he decided he no longer wanted to be a Jefferson County Deputy Sheriff. He's selling his house and moving to a cabin in the country. I envy him. I wish I could retire."

"I think we all look forward to that day," Scott replied in a distracted voice. Deputy Jack's retirement and relocation still concerned him. He forced himself to switch gears. "What about Jeanette? Why are you worried about her? Today's Wednesday. Is she still off sick?" Scott perplexed over what Charly expected of him.

"That's just it…I don't know. I haven't heard from her since Friday. I tried to call her yesterday several times and got no answer. And I've tried to call her several times today. Considering what happened to her husband, Mitch, as I said…I'm a bit worried. I was wondering if you could send a squad car by her house to check on her?" she requested.

Scott sat straight up in his chair now – all of his senses on alert. He did not like the sound of Jeanette being AWOL. Imperative that he find out her whereabouts immediately, he told Charly, "I'll do you one better. I'll go by there myself."

"I'd sure appreciate that," she said, sounding relieved. "When you find her, if you could tell her to give me a call, I'd appreciate that as well."

"I will do that," Scott also promised. He wanted to end this call. He needed to be on his way.

As Scott lowered the receiver, he looked up to see Roger heading back toward his desk. "We need to roll," he told him, leaping to his feet.

"Roll? To where?" Roger questioned, his brow puckered. He had been looking forward to quietly working at his desk for awhile.

"To Jeanette Peterson's. She is AWOL from work since Friday."

"Why don't you just send a squad car to check on her," Roger suggested.

Scott picked up the forensics file and tossed it toward Roger. Roger's reflexes sprung into action, and he reached out and awkwardly caught it. "Read that. It might explain the urgency of checking on Jeanette Peterson's whereabouts," Scott vaguely explained.

He raced past Roger. Looking over his shoulder, Scott's eyes beckoned for Roger to follow. He turned and began moving in Scott's direction. He still had not opened the file yet. He would let Scott drive and browse the report in the car. He hurried to keep up with his long legged partner as he scurried for the door.

* * * *

Having just taken a shower, he stood naked in the bathroom, in his new home. He faced a double vanity with a four-foot mirror above it. Another full-length mirror hung on the door – left there by the previous occupants of the home. He would take this mirror down soon.

He hated looking at his body. It had appalled him since he was a young teen. He thought back on those years now. At fourteen, he discovered he would not develop like other men; he would never lead a normal life.

Worse yet, his sexual appetite was little to none. He experimented with both sexes – hoping one would bring out desire in him. Neither really did much for him. In the end, he stuck with choosing men as sexual partners.

His 'swinging both ways' brought ridicule and hate, and he learned to hate back. His anger finally got the best of him one day. A squirrel chattering at him, taunting from above in a tree had become his outlet.

He spied a forgotten baseball lying in the grass. He picked it up and threw it, with all his might. His aim perfect, the baseball belted the squirrel in the side of the head. The poor animal tumbled, hitting branches as it fell. Finally, it struck the ground with a thud.

As he approached the animal, examining its deceased body – wet, red and brown fur; limp, broken neck; bloody open eye – a perverse pleasure overtook him. Surprised to feel this way, he forced himself to look and walk away. He wanted to feel remorse, but he could not. Quite the opposite, he discovered a sense of peace. *Killing calms the anger.* A bit disconcerting, he had tried to deny this fact.

But the squirrel became the first of hundreds of animals he killed throughout his teen, young adulthood, and subsequent years. The tradeoff for him – ridding the world of a few unwanted animals here and there, versus losing his mind to fury – warranted his loathsome actions.

He never anticipated killing a human being. Renee Peterson's murder changed all that. Now, instead of animals, he hungered to rid the world of a few unwanted human beings as well.

I moved from Kentucky to get away from all that, he reminded himself.

He had left everything behind, including his identity. In this state, he would be known by another name. He had stolen the identity of one of his victims. To the world, this person was among the living again. He had given them life once more.

The killing needs to stop, he told himself. *I need to focus on my new life. The old one doesn't exist anymore.*

He threw on some sweatpants and a T-shirt, and he vacated the bathroom. Tons of boxes to still unpack, he had better things to do but think of his old life. *On with the new!* he decided with determination.

* * * *

Scott pulled the Impala into Jeanette's driveway. As when Roger had brought them there before, the day they told Jeanette about Mitch's death, he pulled the car up in front of the garage. This time, they did not see Jeanette's car through the garage window.

"Shit! It doesn't appear she's home," Scott grumbled, squeezing the top of the steering wheel in frustration.

"Yeah. It looks like her car's gone," Roger concurred. But he released his seatbelt and unlocked his door. "Let's just take a quick look around anyway."

"Okay by me," Scott agreed, slinging his seatbelt off and opening his door.

They both walked toward the patio and the back door. The first thing Scott noticed was the empty patio. "Where's the furniture?" he absently asked. It had been full of furniture when last they had visited.

"Good question," Roger commented, still headed toward the back door.

Scott walked over to the kitchen window instead. As he cupped his hands and prepared to press them to the glass, a wave of nausea shook him. He could not help but think of what he had seen at Debbie's house when he had done this same thing.

Scott swallowed hard and proceeded to press his hands to the glass. When he got a good look at the room, his head snapped back, and he exclaimed, "I can't fuckin' believe this!"

A wave of fury swept over him, and he kicked the brick wall with his shoe. "This can't be happening!"

Roger made his way over to the glass and peeked in as well. "Looks like it has," he commented as he drew back from the window as well, distraught. "Scott, we need to report this."

"I can't believe we let this happen," he lamented.

"There's nothing we can do about it now. We should have been keeping a closer eye out on Jeanette, but we didn't," Roger logically pointed out, angry at himself.

"Shit!" Scott cursed again. *When is this all going to end?*

Roger walked away toward the car. Scott needed a few moments alone. He had every right to be angry. Roger blamed himself. Having turned a blind eye toward Jeanette, he now regretted this decision.

Too late to change anything, all they could do was move forward. They needed to call in what they had discovered. Roger intended to do so right now. He opened the car door, dropped into the driver's seat, picked up the radio receiver, and made a call to headquarters. The sooner they got the ball rolling, the better.

* * * *

He sat in the floor and played with Susanna. A little over a year old now, she walked and said some words – the typical 'dada' and 'mama'. He loved this little girl a great deal – enough to try and change his life for her.

Every inch female, Susanna's ruffled play dress accentuated her girlishness. He loved dressing her in frilly little outfits, and Susanna seemed happy wearing them. She also loved her baby dolls. She had one of them in her arms now, pretending to rock it. *I'm not forcing her to be something she's not*, he was proud to know.

Never liking to be dressed up, his mom had forced him to dress in a manner pleasing to her anyway. As he grew older, he found herself extremely frustrated by his mom's continual efforts to force him to be something he was not. He only wanted to play sports, climb trees, and run with the boys. His mom bought him toys she considered appropriate, but he had no interest in them. He liked trucks and cars.

"My little Susanna doesn't have to worry about things like that," he spoke aloud, bending to kiss Susanna's cheek.

Susanna laughed, smiled, and rose to her feet. She cupped his face in her small hands and kissed him back. "Love you," she said.

"I love Susanna," He replied, feeling warmth in his body.

Susanna smiled once more. Then she toddled back over and picked her doll back up. She went back to playing.

I will do everything to see Susanna has a happy childhood, he privately planned.

A weird day, he found himself reflecting on his childhood a lot. Perhaps it was the gravity of knowing he was a single parent now. Whatever the case, he knew for certain he needed to put Susanna first. His happiness came second to making a good life for this little girl, and that good life came with their new home. It also came with him accepting his new identity.

His genetic makeup said he was a man, and in his heart, he knew she was. But outwardly he appeared female. Breast implants created the illusion even more.

Reifenstein Syndrome they called it. This disorder made his life a living hell. Born a boy, he always appeared to be a girl. The illness meant his body rejected all male hormones. He had always felt like a boy – playing with boys and enjoying their games. But because he looked like a girl, his mom had tried to force him to act like one and had been disturbed by his odd, male behavior. His dad tried to play it off saying, "She's a tomboy. She'll outgrow it."

But his teen years brought more heartache. When he did not start menstruating, the truth reared its ugly head. At first, doctors thought he had a tumor. The 'tumor' was discovered to be undeveloped, un-descended testicles. He also had no womb or ovaries. DNA testing revealed he was male.

His parents refused to accept this 'nonsense'. Jeanette was their daughter, not their son. They expected her to go on with her life as a woman. They put her through surgery to remove the useless male genitalia. Doctors actually recommended this procedure, because a high likelihood of testicular cancer loomed if the undeveloped testicles remained.

His parents also approved breast augmentation surgery. They wanted their daughter to look like a woman. They believed adding this enhancement would make Jeanette feel like a woman and be able to lead a woman's life. But Jeanette found acting in this manner impossible. She felt like a freak of nature.

He began to experiment sexually and discovered he had no sex drive. Lack of hormones caused this situation to be a reality as well. He grew more and more disheartened and irate.

Killing became an outlet for him. But as he watched people leading normal lives, he still could not escape the insufferable envy he felt. When he and Renee struck up a friendship, and Renee revealed she was not happy with her 'normal' life, it was more than Jeanette could stand. He saw Mitch and Susanna as his ticket to a happy, 'normal' life.

And so he had killed his first human being. The overall satisfaction, and mock sexual rush, he received led him to commit more murders. Mitch's selfish, overwhelming sexual desires led him to kill Mitch as well.

The one thing right with his life was being a mommy to precious Susanna. Susanna only wanted to be loved. A determined Jeanette would provide this love to this little girl.

Many single parent homes existed. So in a way, his life was still 'normal'. But he could *not* keep killing. Sooner or later, the police would catch up with him. *And then who would Susanna have?*

So Jeanette made up his mind to stay one step in front of the detectives. He collected life insurance from Mitch – $200,000 – more than enough to set up house in another state. Just as an added precaution, Jeanette also decided to change his identity. He even colored his hair – jet black – no more redhead. Even if the police should stumble onto something pinning him to the murders in Kentucky, they would not recognize or be able to find him.

Killing is over. Being a full-time mom is my focus now. I'm now a woman. The world doesn't know any different, and they never will.

"Mama," Susanna called. She held out a plastic, star-shaped block to Jeanette.

"Mama's here, Sus. Mama will always be here."

Jeanette took the block from her daughter's outstretched hand and showed Susanna what hole it fit into. Then he handed it back to Susanna and watched as she pushed it in. Clapping and smiling at his daughter, he encouraged her intelligence. "We're going to have a good life here, Susanna," he told her.

"Mama," she replied, handing her another plastic shape.

Jeanette took it from her with a smile. *Life is good!* he concluded. Being a mother had to be enough to make him happy. Killing was done…he hoped.

Chapter 31

Can't Let It Go

Scott still reeled from the sight of Jeanette's empty house, so Roger offered to drive back to the station. Scott let him. He feared he would ram the car into something if he drove. His anger ate at him like acid. *I played with Jeanette too much. She knew we were on to her, so she skipped town. How could I have been so stupid?!*

"Scott, I'm sorry," Roger told him, once they were underway.

"You're sorry?" he questioned. "For what?"

"For not believing in you. Jeanette might be in jail right now if I had listened to you. You were right all along. It's all starting to make sense now. Jeanette killed Renee to step into her life. I think she killed Chad an... and...Debbie...because she had easy access to them, and they trusted her. As to Mitch, I guess she didn't like being married to him after all. Now, I'm worried about that precious little girl. She may have already killed her...."

"God...I hope not," Scott said with despair, rubbing his forehead. "I don't think this is your fault, Roger. I think I did this. I taunted Jeanette the last time I talked to her...when I gathered her DNA sample. I bought her a soft drink, and I kept the straw. I must have gone too far. I should have kept my big

218

mouth shut. I don't know what I was thinking. It was like I believed I could goad her into a confession or something. How stupid is that?"

"Well...we wouldn't even have her DNA right now if you hadn't come up with the ingenious plan to steal her straw. I wondered how you got her DNA...without a warrant. I didn't figure she voluntarily submitted it. The guilty usually are smart enough not to do that. And Jeanette appears to be plenty guilty...and plenty smart. She kept one step ahead of us by vacating her house."

"Shit!" Scott cussed again. "We've got to track her down, Roger. She'll keep killing. She gets a thrill from this."

"I agree," he said, glancing at his young partner. Roger had a new respect for Scott now. Scott's tenaciousness had irritated him to no end. But because of it, they had identified a serial killer. Now, they just needed to find her. "There's an APB out on her. If she is still in the state, maybe we'll catch a break."

"I don't think she's still in the state," Scott stated in a quiet, defeated voice.

"Well...even if she isn't, we'll get her," Roger said with more confidence than he felt.

"What about Stacy?" Scott suddenly asked.

A strange question, Roger responded with another question, "What about her?"

"She didn't kill Chad. Jeanette did. Will they drop the charges against her?"

"I doubt it," Roger admitted. "They still have damning evidence against her. It will be up to her defense attorney to argue she's been wrongly accused."

"So she'll still have to stand trial?"

"I'm sure she will. If her DNA was not on the clothes with Chad's blood on them, she might be able to walk. But it is…"

"That has to be a mistake," Scott argued. "It didn't feel right when we arrested her. I think she told us the truth. The only part she had in Chad's death was finding him dead and not reporting it."

"You may be right, but that's for a defense attorney to convince a jury now," Roger stated the facts.

These facts brought Scott even more unrest. *There's a possibility an innocent girl might go to prison for something a monster did.*

"Scott, there is only so much we can do. We're governed by the legal system. We just have to hope the scales of justice work, and if Stacy is truly innocent, she will be set free."

"And what's our next step in tracking down the real killer – Jeanette?"

"We'll talk to her neighbors. If she moved all the furniture, chances are she had a moving company help her. If this is the case, there should have been a moving truck in her driveway. If we can get an ID on what moving company, we can get a court order to pull their records. Then we should be able to track down where they moved the stuff to. If she's in another state, she will have to be extradited. But at least we'll have her in custody somewhere."

"And if no one saw a moving truck?"

"Then we may have to do the America's Most Wanted thing and have her picture posted on television and wait for tips."

"And that can take months…or even years," Scott stated with disgust, shaking his head and blowing out his lips.

"We'll get her Scott. I don't know when, but we'll get her."

And how many other loved ones will die while we wait for information to come in? Scott pondered in agony, his heart aching for Debbie again. He was silent the rest of the ride back to the station.

* * * *

When Scott walked in the next morning, Roger got a start when he glimpsed the clothes he donned – a short, casual jacket, jeans, and a T-shirt. "What's up?" he asked, his face scrunched.

Scott reached in one pocket of his coat and pulled forth his gun. He reached in the other and extracted his badge. He laid both on the desk in front of Roger.

"Scott, what are you doing?" Roger inquired. Pressing the palms of his hands against the arms of his chair, he gave his partner a hard, concerned stare.

"Any news on Jeanette Peterson's whereabouts?" Scott questioned.

"No...not yet. It will take some time. But we'll track her down," Roger assured once more.

"You guys keep right on with your investigation," Scott encouraged. "But I can't be a part of it."

"What are you talking about?" Roger asked. He tapped his fingers together now with nervous energy.

"I need results, Roger. I can't let Jeanette run free for years on end. God only knows how many more people she could kill..."

"Scott, you can't go off half cocked..." Roger began to argue.

"I don't intend to," Scott assured him. "I thought long and hard about this last night. Searching for Jeanette on the force, I'll have to follow all kinds of rules. If I search for her as a private investigator, it opens up a lot more freedoms. I've got to find her, Roger, and see she is brought to justice for what she has done. I've got to do this for Debbie."

Silence reigned for a few moments. Roger still intently stared at Scott. He knew how stubborn he could be when he made up his mind about something. This stubborn streak had lead to him gathering Jeanette's DNA. As he had told Scott yesterday, if he had not gone out on a limb and tested her, they still would not know who the killer was.

"I can tell your mind is made up," Roger stated, cheerless. "The department will be losing one hell of a detective. And I hate to lose the best partner I've had in a long time."

"Thanks, Roger," Scott said, giving him a slight smile of appreciation. "Maybe I'll be as good of a PI and I'll track Jeanette down within a week or two. Then I can call this a leave of absence and come back on duty."

"I hope it goes that way," Roger said, his statement genuine. He truly did hate to lose Scott as his partner. "Good luck, buddy. You call me if I can do anything to help."

"Will do," Scott promised.

He offered his hand to Roger. Roger gave him a firm handshake and a half smile. Squeezing his hand, he advised, "Keep your wits about you. This woman is very dangerous."

"Yes, she is," Scott agreed. "And I don't intend to let her get the better of me. I'll get her for you guys, Roger. We've got to get her put away. You do what you can to help Stacy Prescott out, okay?"

"Will do," he promised. Roger still was not sure whether Stacy Prescott was guilty or not. He was inclined to think she was *not* now, but the evidence still seemed to suggest otherwise. He knew her father would hire the best defense attorneys available, so Roger only hoped her legal team worked their magic.

"I'll see you around, Roger," Scott said.

"See ya, kid," Roger said in conclusion, looking down at his desk.

Scott turned then and headed for the door. As he passed the painted wall that said Criminal Investigations Unit, he thought with pride, *It was nice being a part of this.* He smiled and waved at the receptionist. On the phone, she could not speak to him, but she smiled and waved back. Scott walked out the door, allowing it to close softly behind him.

I'm doing what I need to, Scott told himself, as he pushed the down button on elevator panel. *I've got to see Jeanette is caught and justice is done. I have to see this killer is incarcerated so she can't hurt anyone else.*

The elevator arrived and Scott stepped aboard. He was on his way to bringing Jeanette Peterson to justice. He was determined to stop this maniac's insane killing spree. *Debbie, I'll see justice is done for you,* he promised once again. His lingering love for his sweet, departed Debbie would keep him focused and on task. *Look out, Jeanette, here I come!*

The End

Continue the journey....

You have just completed **Sissy Marlyn's** first murder mystery. Don't despair! There will be more engrossing novels to lose yourself in from **Sissy Marlyn**.

Still planned for 2006: *Jury Pool – A Killer's Mind*. Having enjoyed *Jury Pool – Summons...to Die*, you will want to pick up the next novel in this series. Discover what happens to Jeanette and Susanna in their new lives and if Scott ever tracks them down. Planned release date: September 2006.

Women's Fiction Fans, also, be on the lookout for the first novel in the *Bluegrass* Series, beginning with book number one entitled: *Bardstown*. Planned release date: July 2006.

And just for fun, don't forget about the "Identify the "*T*" Trilogy Character" Contest that will be posted on **Sissy Marlyn's** website – www.sissymarlyn.com. The first reader to tell me the name of the character, from the "*T*" trilogy, and the page this character appears on, in *Jury Pool – Summons...to Die* and *Bardstown*, could win a special prize.

Check the **Sissy Marlyn** website **www.sissy marlyn. com** often for updates on upcoming novels and contest information.

Thank you!

Sissy Marlyn

Printed in the United States
49619LVS00003B/229-294